&FAIRY STORIES FAIRY STORIES

Traditional tales for children,
Contemporary tales for adults

Clive Johnson

Labyrinthe Press
www.labyrinthepublishers.com

Labyrinthe Press
Leigh-on-Sea, United Kingdom
www.labyrinthepublishers.com

Publisher's Note: This is a work of fiction. Names, characters, places, and incidents are a product of the author's or original storyteller's imagination. Locales and public names are sometimes used for atmospheric purposes. Any association with actual people, living or dead, or to organisations, events, or institutions, is unintentional.

Book Layout ©2013 BookDesignTemplates.com
Cover illustration © iStock/sSplajn
Cover format by Jacqueline Abromeit
Distributed by Ingram

British Library Cataloguing in Publication Data
Fairy Stories & Fairy Stories/ Clive Johnson. —2nd ed.
ISBN 978-0-9932029-8-8 (Print edition)
ISBN 978-0-9932029-9-5 (Electronic edition)
Also available as an audible digital audiobook.

Please note that the traditional tales in this book (the first chapter in each part) are suitable for children. All other stories are intended for adult readers, and are not suitable for children.

To my mother, who first taught me about wolves, and witches, and pigs that can speak.

CONTENTS

Introduction

Fairy stories have the capacity to grip the imagination and stir the soul no less powerfully than did the myths of gods, goddesses, and heroes for earlier generations. The stories may have been intended for children, yet are capable of arousing fresh interest and teaching important truths for anyone.

Many of the tales that are most familiar to western readers–notably the stories written by Wilhelm and Jacob Grimm–are retellings of earlier stories. There is a risk when updating a story, for, as the Austro-American psychologist Bruno Bettelheim puts it: "Unless he is an original artist, an author recasting a fairy tale is rarely guided mainly by his unconscious feeling for the story...changes are most often instituted on the basis of what the author thinks a 'general' reader wishes to be told."[1]

At the same time, when it is given careful attention, a new telling can be more powerful than the first. Few managed this task as admirably as the Grimm brothers, who continually updated their stories over a period of more than forty years.

While tales of beautiful princesses and enchanting castles, animals that can speak, and witches and fairies who work magic might enthral a young child, a good fairy story always contains an important message, which a young listener or reader would do well to take notice of.

The teaching for a child may be about the challenges that they are likely to face as they grow up, about understanding their relationship with others, or offer a warning that will help prepare them in their looming sexual development. While subconsciously their processing of the deeper teaching of a story might be unsettling, they are helped to prepare for the realities of life that they will face as they move toward adulthood.

In each case, a fairy story touches something deep, imparting its message using images and metaphors in a way that might otherwise be difficult to put into words.

---

[1] Bettelheim, B. (1976), *The Uses of Enchantment: The meaning and importance of fairy tales*, New York: Vintage Books (2010 edition), p 215.

As the early twentieth-century essayist Hamilton Wright Mabie puts it, a fairy story is "a spontaneous and instinctive endeavour to shape the facts of the world to meet the needs of the imagination, the cravings of the heart."[2] These are stories that connect with universal knowledge, with archetypes, and with the Divine.

A child knows instinctively when a leading protagonist in a story is in danger. I can well remember being taken to the cinema by my grandfather to see the classic 1937 Disney telling of the *Snow White* story, and needing to hide under my seat when Snow White accepted the poisoned apple from the evil queen. It was immediately obvious to me what was happening. I'm sure that most children will have had similar experiences; the tricks and sub-plots that are played out in a story that stirs the soul don't need to be spelled out.

My intention with the stories that are presented here is to bring alive the messages of some of the great fairy tales that might not be obvious for a young child. Many of these are no less relevant for older readers, and so the stories that follow my retelling of each familiar tale speak specifically to an adult audience.

This is a domain in which being lost in a world can be interpreted as a journey into the unknown subcon-

---

[2] Mabie, H. W. (ed.) (1905), *Fairy Tales Every Child Should Know*, Doubleday, Doran & Inc.

scious, where wolves represent the shadow aspects of ourselves that might seek to ensnare us, and where princes and princesses allude to a higher way of living. In referring to experiences that we might relate to, the intention of these stories is, to borrow the words of sociologist Arthur W. Frank, "to animate human life; that is their work. [They] work with people, for people, and always stories work on people, affecting what people are able to see as real, as possible, and as worth doing or best avoided."[3]

The discoveries, conflicts, rewards of virtuous behaviour, and major transitions through life that are described by the Grimms, Hans Christian Andersen, Charles Perrault and others often actually do occur in the real world. Each of the partner stories to the classic tales that are included here attempt to illustrate such possibilities.

Many have sought to offer interpretations for the different tales. Among the most common of these are those who examine the needs for a healthy psychosexual development, and those who look for a religious meaning in the writing. However, it's usually the case that no one interpretation can adequately reveal the richness in any one story. The ability of these timeless tales to allow for different perspectives and support

---

[3] Frank, A. W. (2010), *Letting Stories Breathe: A socio-narratology*, University of Chicago Press, p 3.

many different levels of meaning is a part of what makes them so magical.

I have offered some threads of thinking behind my retelling of the stories, but these should by no means be considered to be the only interpretations that might be suggested. Far more detailed analysis and explanation is offered by the likes of well-known guides to the classic tales, such as Bettelheim, Murphy and Zipes.[4]

The versions of the tales that I have chosen to include tend to be those that I believe will be best known by most readers. There are significant differences in the content of some stories, and some authors even worked with several versions of the same tale. For example, the Grimm brothers' *Little Red Cap* is followed by a sequel, incorporating aspects of a second version of the *Red Riding Hood* story that had been told to them. Their version of this same tale sees Little Red Cap and her grandmother being freed from the wolf's belly; the earlier story by Charles Perrault has them both being devoured. The experience depicted in my

---

[4] See, for example, Bettelheim, B. (1976), *op. cit.*, Murphy, G. R. (2000), *The Owl, The Raven, And The Dove: The religious meaning of the Grimms' magic fairy tales*, Oxford University Press, and Zipes, J. (2012), *The Irresistible Fairy Tale: The cultural and social history of a genre*, Princeton University Press.

modern-day interpretation is similarly intended to be shocking and disturbing.

Different storytellers may change names, settings, and cultural references, although without affecting a story's underlying meaning. This is yet another way in which the fairy tale can be compared to a classical myth, and perhaps also to a story that might as easily be found in a holy book such as *The Bible* or *The Bhagavad Gita*.

Some adaptations of old stories that have been made by later tellers appear to have resulted from a wish to dumb down some of the cruelty and violence that appeared in the original. The Grimms' sparing of Little Red Cap may be one example of this. However, skilful authors such as the Grimms are able to retain the often dark and cautioning realities of life that most stories attend to—not all fairy tales have happy endings.

As an adult reading a story to a child, it's tempting to ignore the powerful teaching that a tale provides. With a mature perspective, and appreciating that what's being told is not all pure fantasy, I believe that any reader, however old, can discover new meaning and wonder in these classic tales. This is perhaps the reason why these great stories have continued to inspire and enthral generation after generation.

The Sleeping Beauty

In a distant time, there lived a king and queen who were content with their lives, but for the fact that they lacked a child.

"Oh my dear husband!" the queen exclaimed most days, "If only we had a child!"

The king could barely console his wife, for he dearly yearned for a daughter or a son too.

By a miracle, the queen eventually did fall heavy with a child. She gave birth to a beautiful daughter, whose pure skin and pretty eyes enthralled all who saw her.

The king was so overjoyed by this precious gift, that he ordered a splendid feast to celebrate the miracle that had happened. Royal relatives were invited to the celebration, along with wise women from across the kingdom.

Now, it happened that there were thirteen wise women living in the kingdom, but the royal castle only had twelve golden plates on which to serve them food. And so, only twelve of the wise women were invited to the feast.

The banquet was a splendid affair. The finest food was served, and everyone who came was in joyful spirit.

When the dining was over, each of the wise women stepped forward in turn to present the baby princess with a special gift.

The first brought her the gift of virtue, so that she might grow up to have the finest morals. The second bestowed upon her the gift of beauty, such that others might always wonder at her. The next promised her the gift of great riches, so that she would never lack for anything. And so, each of the wise women came forward to offer their gifts, until the eleventh of them had spoken.

At this point, without warning, the wise woman who had not been invited to the feast stormed into the banqueting hall. She was furious that she had been left out of the invitations to the party, and swore vengeance on the newborn child.

"And here is my gift!" she roared without taking a moment to acknowledge those who were gathered around. "I swear that in her fifteenth year, this little child will prick her finger on a spindle, and will drop down dead!"

Having spoken her wicked words, the evil woman charged out of the castle, leaving everyone astonished by what they had heard.

After a time, the twelfth wise woman stepped forward. She hadn't yet made her gift before the wicked woman had thundered into the castle.

"I cannot reverse this curse," she began. "But I can soften its blow. The princess will not die as our wicked intruder decreed, but rather will fall into a deep sleep. After one hundred years, when the time is right, a king's son will visit the castle, and his kiss will awaken the dear child."

The king and queen were overcome with grief after hearing the threat of the scorned woman, but found some comfort in the gift offered by the twelfth of those who had been invited to the great feast.

After that day, the king did everything in his power to prevent his daughter from befalling the terrible misfortune that had been promised her. He ordered that all of the spindles in the kingdom be destroyed, and vowed that his daughter should not even come to know that such devices had ever existed.

As the princess grew older, each of the gifts that had been promised to her began to be realised. She became modest and sweet natured, virtuous in her manner, and more beautiful by the day.

On the day that she turned fifteen, it happened that the king and queen needed to be away from the castle for a short time. Left alone, the princess decided to explore the many parts of the castle that she had never visited before. She pushed at doors leading into unknown chambers and secret closets, and wandered along corridors that she'd not seen before.

One small door that she pushed open revealed a very steep, narrow staircase, which seemed to wind its way up high into a tall tower. "How exciting!" thought the princess to herself, "I must find out where this staircase leads to!"

She climbed the many steps that spiralled up through the tower, lifting the long skirt of her dress as she did so, to avoid tripping over herself. When she reached the top of the staircase, she came upon another small door. Curious, she turned its knob, and peered around the door to see what lay beyond it.

She saw a small room, and at its centre sat an old woman, who was spinning flax on a spindle.

"Oh, this looks very exciting!" cried the princess. "What is this strange instrument that you are working with?" she asked the old woman.

"This is a spindle, my dear," replied the old woman. "I am using it to spin flax. Come and see!"

The princess stepped toward the spindle and gently let her hand explore its slender frame. No sooner had she done this, than she pricked her finger on the fine spike of its tail, and as had been foretold, immediately fell into a deep sleep.

In the great hall of the castle below her, everyone else fell asleep too. The king and queen, who had just returned from their outing, fell silent on their thrones. The whole court froze exactly where they were, as though time had suddenly stood still. In the kitchen, the cook stopped right at the moment that she was about to beat the scullery boy with a rolling pin. Close by, a maid froze in the very state she was in when plucking a hen for that night's supper.

Even the flies on the wall fell silent, and the flickering of the fire below the great chimney turned to stillness.

In the castle stables, the horses yawned and were soon fast asleep. Pigeons that were perched on the castle walls fell into a deep sleep too–just as everyone else who was in the castle.

Soon, a wild thistle bush grew up around the castle. The bush grew so quickly and so tall, that before long it was impossible to see the castle behind it. The hedge became impenetrable even for the most valiant of the many young men who tried to fight their way through it. At first, many tried, and later others who had watched them, while biding their time until making attempts of their own. All ended up being torn to shreds by its knife-sharp thorns.

After some time, no one attempted to reach the castle any more. After still more years, the people of the kingdom even began to forget that there once was a castle that had drawn great attention from across the land.

Very many years later, a young prince from a foreign land journeyed to the kingdom. He met an old man, who told him stories about the forgotten castle, and the beautiful princess who was said to still be sleeping there.

The prince was enthralled by what he was told, and became determined to discover for himself whether the tales were true.

Now, it happened that exactly one hundred years had passed since the princess and the household of the castle fell asleep. So when the prince approached the hedge of thorns that the old man told him about, he instead discovered a pretty bush of flowers, which opened a pathway for him, such that he could pass through to the castle without being harmed. As soon as he had made his passage, the bush again closed up behind him.

As he entered the castle grounds, the prince saw the pigeons that were perched like statues on the castle walls, and then saw the horses that didn't stir, standing without moving in their stables. Everything lay silent, as quiet as it's possible to be.

Once inside the castle, the prince saw the flies that were stuck to the walls as though lifeless. He saw the maid, and the scullery boy, and the cook, and the whole court–all frozen in the manner that they had been when the princess first touched the spindle. Next, he saw the king and queen, asleep on their thrones.

The prince was amazed at what he found, continuing to explore all over the castle. Eventually, he found the small doorway that led to the steep, narrow staircase that had led the princess to the room at the top of the tower.

The prince followed the same route that she had taken many years before, finally arriving at the small room in which the princess lay asleep. As he quietly pulled open the door, he could barely believe what he saw before him.

"How beautiful she is!" he exclaimed to himself. "Never before have I seen one so fair and charming!"

Unable to fix his glance on anything else, the prince bent down beside the princess, and gently kissed her forehead.

Immediately, the princess woke up, seemingly as though nothing had happened. She saw the prince smiling sweetly at her, and she was at once in love with the fine man who had rescued her.

The prince related the strange story to her that the old man had told him, and then both he and the princess descended the long staircase to see what might have happened elsewhere in the castle.

To their great delight, the castle was alive once more. The king and queen had awoken where they were sitting. The whole court had begun going about their business as though nothing had happened. In the kitchen, the cook's rolling pin cracked firmly onto the back of the head of the scullery boy, and the maid carried on plucking the hen, just as she had been doing many years before. The fire below the great chimney started flickering again, billowing ash and roaring loudly, just as it had done when it was magically stilled.

The flies that had been motionless started buzzing around, and in the castle stables, the horses joined together in a chorus of loud neighing. Even the pigeons that perched on the castle walls started cooing again.

The king and queen were overjoyed to see their daughter again, and everyone was happy to be setting about their business as they had done before.

The prince and princess grew ever more in love, and soon they were married in a grand ceremony at the castle. Together, they lived contentedly for the rest of their days.

Sleep in heavenly peace

Every family that lived through the war has a story to tell. Mine is no different. We lived in a canal house in Delfshaven, a busy little place on the west side of Rotterdam.

I was born just after the beginning of the Great Depression, a time of great hardship for everyone. My family fared better than most–my father was a doctor, and while the money that he earned was barely enough to pay for bread and milk, his job was safe, and we came through the worst of that terrifying time. We were helped by a regular supply of vegetables that my grandmother used to pick for us, proudly grown in her smallholding, which she kept just north of the city.

I was the youngest of four boys, all living at home at the time. Jan, my eldest brother, was in his final year at school when I started at kindergarten. After finishing his basic education, he planned to find work for a while, before going on to university at Groningen, a city in the far north of the Netherlands.

Ours was a very close family. Mother and Father were the best of parents, always playing games and making things for us kids. Papa often used to take us to fly a kite in the park, while Mama seemed to spend her whole life baking heavenly cakes for us to eat.

I loved my early years, and I think that my family was the happiest that I knew. We made do with what we had, knowing that we were much better off than most.

Before the depression, my parents had enjoyed collecting fine china ornaments, and also had a good sense for buying elegant paintings. In some ways, our house was like a small art gallery, which gave me many opportunities to wonder at the beauty of the treasures that adorned our home.

While they dearly loved us boys, my parents really wanted to have a daughter. My sister Hannah was born when I was two, meaning that I was no longer the youngest in the family. Hannah's arrival completed my parents' happiness. We had almost everything that we needed, and we had each other.

The church was packed for Hannah's christening. My parents had asked as many people as they could to join them, and all of these many guests were afterwards invited to a grand meal that my mother had prepared. I don't remember that day, but everyone was still talking about it for many years to come.

My earliest memory is of a Christmastime, when I'd turned five, and had been given my first bike as a special present. All of a sudden, I felt that I was the king of the road, or at least the king of our little street. Mama often used to warn me not to race so fast up and down the narrow cobbled pathway, which ran alongside the canal. But other than the odd tumble, I never came to injury.

Things were sadly different for my little sister when she reached my age. She'd been given an old tricycle, which had once belonged to the daughter of one of our neighbours, Mrs. Van den Berg. My parents had been surprised by this gift, since Mrs. Van den Berg had never been friendly toward our family before, always accusing us kids of making too much noise, or annoying her dog, or nearly knocking her down on the street. She'd not been invited to Hannah's christening– a decision that was bound to have upset her.

Still, Hannah's tricycle was gratefully received, and soon put into busy action. Hannah loved her bike, as I loved mine. It was her favourite thing, apart from a delicately painted china doll that our brother Jan had bought for her.

Jan was now working at a warehouse on the other side of the Maas. Soon, he would be leaving our home to begin his studies in Groningen. He was particularly fond of his young sister, and she adored him.

When Jan left home to start his degree, Hannah didn't stop crying for days. "I want Big Jan back!" she screamed, "Come back and play with Little Hannah and Hannah's friend!"

Jan promised to come back to visit us during his holidays, and at least until the war started, he was faithful to his word.

For the next year or two, life continued much as it had always done. Hannah and I raced against each other on our bikes, Mother baked cakes and Father looked after his patients. We were happy. But a monstrous tragedy was soon to beset our family.

Hannah and I were out playing with our bikes as usual, when suddenly, the chain of her tricycle stuck fast against the teeth of the bike's chain ring. We had never known anything like this before, and never learned how this peculiar incident occurred.

Hannah pushed down firmly on the pedals in an effort to free the chain, but to no avail. She stood down on the pedals to put as much of her body weight into her tread as she could, her hands pushing against the handlebars in an effort to balance herself. But rather than freeing the chain, she was sent flying right over the top of the bike, landing sharply on the hard cobble stones of the street in front of her.

The way that Hannah landed could not have been worse. She had had no time to prepare herself to cushion her fall, and landed squarely on her head. I raced toward her, screaming for help. Passers-by quickly rushed over to where Hannah lay, one of whom alerted my mother, who came running from our house.

The wheels of the bike were still spinning, temporarily mesmerising me as if I'd lost all sense of time. Hannah's accident seemed unreal to me in that moment, and it was only some time later that I came to terms with the full impact of what had happened.

A small trickle of blood issued from Hannah's forehead, but it was the large bruises that were forming around her temples that most caught my attention.

Hannah was completely silent, not uttering a murmur. At first I thought that she might be dead, but my mother assured me that she was still breathing. Looking at her face, I could see why everyone thought that she was so beautiful. She seemed to me to be totally pure, so innocent. I loved my little sister, and longed that she would soon be back playing with me.

Hannah was taken to hospital, and my father was called. He suspected right away that she'd suffered a brain injury. This was soon confirmed by the doctors who cared for her at the hospital.

"I'm very sorry to inform you, Dr. and Mrs. De Jong," The senior doctor in charge of Hannah's care told my parents, "That your daughter has suffered a

severe brain injury. We fear that she will not recover
from her coma, but we cannot say how much longer she
may live."

My parents couldn't believe what they had heard,
but they immediately resolved to make sure that Hannah was kept as comfortable as possible, choosing to
nurse her at home. Father's profession equipped him
well for knowing how best to care for her.

Hannah came home with us to stay one week later.
My mother placed her favourite doll on her pillow, the
one that Jan had bought her. It never left her side. We
all took turns to just be with her, holding her hand,
and telling her that we loved her. She never opened her
eyes nor showed any sign of hearing us, but I believed
what Mama had said, that even though she couldn't
speak to us, in her heart she knew that we were with
her.

As I approached my tenth birthday, the tranquil
world that we'd known before Hannah's accident was
to be dealt another crushing blow. We'd heard on the
nightly radio broadcasts that our neighbour Germany
had set about invading what it believed were territories
belonging to the German people. Great Britain and
France declared war on Germany toward the end of the
year, after the Nazis had invaded Poland.

We listened to the crackly broadcasts from Hilver-
sum with great interest, but Father assured us that
Holland was safe. Our country had proclaimed itself

neutral when the Allies started their campaign, and Hitler had promised to respect our sovereignty.

To start with, nothing much seemed to change. We didn't at first see many bombers passing over our skies, carrying their deadly cargoes to and fro' across the sea. The news stories reported that the French and the British were dragging their feet about launching a full offensive on Germany.

Still, Mother and Father believed that it wouldn't be long before our simple lives would be rudely interrupted by everything that was happening around us. Most people in our street thought that we were mad when we set about converting the third storey of our house to look as though it were our attic room, which actually was on the fourth floor. My parents' concern was so great for Hannah. They especially feared that if any foreign army rampaged through our city, Hannah might be discovered and abused.

The conversion was cleverly done. Two sharply angled wooden eaves created an impression of supporting the roof, whereas in fact, each concealed a small space to its side. What looked like a single, boarded-up window was crafted into the woodwork at each end of the room. We placed a stepladder behind one side of the false ceiling, allowing us to climb up to the real attic room, since the original staircase between the third and fourth storeys had been removed.

A very small gap at the bottom of one of the angled panels was in fact a handle, which we could pull upon to open up a small trapdoor that was built into the eave. We could thus crawl into the small space that lay behind, and then climb up the stepladder to reach the upper room.

Despite our Prime Minister's promises that we were safe from invasion, Hitler renegaded on his agreement, ordering troops to be sent into our country without warning in the spring of 1940.

The march of the Nazis was breathtakingly fast. On the first day of the invasion, German paratroopers had landed near The Hague, but our forces on the ground had managed to prevent their attempt to seize our air-fields.

As a major seaport, Rotterdam was especially vulnerable. In fact, the Germans also arrived here on the very first day of their campaign, landing seaplanes on the Maas. The tiny garrison that was stationed here bravely tried to protect the city, but it was quickly is-sued with an ultimatum by the German commander– either our troops surrendered, or he would bomb the city.

Our commander wasn't even allowed to see a signed copy of the ultimatum before the bombing began. Against all expectation, the Luftwaffe aimed directly at the areas of the city where people were living. In a single night, nearly one thousand people lost their lives. Tens of thousands more were left homeless.

Given the unexpected arrival of the bombers over our city, and Hannah's uncompromising situation, we felt we had no option but to stay put in our home. We crouched for protection under Father's old worktable, which occupied most of the ground floor.

All night, we heard the drone of the Luftwaffe all around us. The sounds that I heard will stay with me for as long as I live. Screaming bomb after screaming bomb pounded the city, setting off explosions that were so loud that I thought my eardrums would burst. We heard desperate people crying out for their lives, and tasted the smoke of distant fires that had broken out at various warehouses along the dockside.

When the night was over, the full terror of what the Nazi's onslaught had brought was immediately obvious. By a miracle, our neighbourhood had been spared from the bombing, but we could see plumes of smoke towering into the sky in the distance, and soon learned that much of the centre of the city had been totally destroyed.

Many people had managed to escape their homes in the days preceding the bombing, when the Luftwaffe had already made a show of force. Father and Mother took in one family that had fled their home, who now shared our small space and dwindling food supply.

The newcomers helped us to move Hannah's bed
into the upper attic room, which also became a storage
area for the fine ornaments and paintings that had
brightened our rooms. Mother and Father didn't want
any unwelcome visitors laying their hands on their
valuable collection, fearing that their beloved artworks
might easily be looted.

Our country was forced to surrender to Germany
just a few days after the bombardment of our city. The
Nazis had threatened to let loose their terror on the
city of Utrecht if we did not, and our army was too
small to offer any realistic resistance.

The Nazis quickly took control of our country, setting about a policy that aimed to convert us to their
evil creed. A German master was put in charge of our
school, and a swastika flag was placed in a prominent
position at the front of each classroom.

As a young boy, my life was less affected by the
takeover than were the lives of many. I did as I was
told, especially promising my parents not to tell anyone
about our secret hideaway. Father assured me that we
could trust the family that we'd taken into our home,
who were good people that were known to him. However, we were forbidden to talk freely with anyone else.

Hannah knew nothing of what was happening–at
least, we didn't believe that she could know. We often
grouped together around her bed, chatting to her as
though she were still conscious. Mother and Father

promised that one of them would always stay near her, whatever happened. Often, we would sit staring at her radiant face, remembering the happy times that we'd once shared.

Jan wrote to us from Groningen once in a while, but his letters started to become less and less frequent as the war gathered pace. He'd been forced to give up his studies to work in a factory, making aircraft parts for the Luftwaffe. Every man under a certain age had been forced into similar work. My father only escaped being taken away from his patients because he was older than the qualifying age at the time.

We didn't know if we would see Jan again. There was no sign either that Hannah might ever come out of her coma.

Many of our friends who the Nazis regarded as not being a part of their so-called "master race" were forced to wear badges that marked them out from the rest of us. My Jewish friends at school were among them. Their parents had been forced out of their jobs, and they were often pushed around and sworn at by the soldiers who'd moved in to the city.

We learned to survive on a very meagre diet. All food was rationed, although my grandmother still managed to hide some of her vegetables for us, defying the Nazi's order that all produce must to be given up for the war effort. We knew that if anyone found out, she would be severely punished.

One day, about two years after our city had been bombed, my Jewish friends didn't turn up for school any more. I never saw them again.

We continued with our lives as best we could, thinking that the nightmare that we were living through would never end. The radio news reported that the Nazis were close to victory, but we never knew who or what we could believe.

We managed, at least, to stay together as a family. Even though Jan was far away, the precious china doll that he'd given to Hannah–her favourite toy that never moved from her side–was our way of believing that he was still present with us.

As the war wore on, the fortune of the Allies suddenly seemed to take a dramatic turn for the better. We heard on the BBC that the Western Allies had succeeded in landing thousands of troops on the beaches of Normandy. Their arrival at our border was, we thought, only a matter of days away. We heard that a town in the south-east of the country had been freed by the Allies, but they weren't successful in securing the bridges that crossed the major rivers in the east, despite making what we later learned was the largest drop of paratroopers during the whole war.

Another battle raged near the city of Antwerp some hundred kilometres to our south, and this time, the Allies' mission succeeded. But it soon became clear that the country wasn't going to be liberated quite as quickly as we'd hoped.

The winter that arrived at the end of the fifth year of the Nazi's occupation became by far the worse time that we faced since that first night of bombing. The Nazis had stopped allowing food to be sent to us, following a strike by our railway workers. What became known as the *Hongerwinter* took the lives of tens of thousands of people.

Our ration coupons could no longer buy us meat. Very soon, only the smallest amount of bread and a tiny handful of potatoes were all that were left on the shelves of the grocery store. Grandmother still managed to smuggle one or two vegetables to us when she could, but it's no mistake to say that we were very close to starving.

The Nazis had also banned fuel from being sent to us. Some people became so cold, that they had to use the furniture in their homes as firewood. We huddled together in the attic room whenever we could, wrapping as many layers of clothing around us that we could lay our hands on. Through all of this, Hannah stayed sleeping.

The famine lasted for many months, but as the Allies gradually made progress in pushing the Nazis back, the British and Canadian air forces were eventually allowed to make drops of food over our area of Holland, which eased our situation a little.

The Allied forces again tried to capture the Rhine crossings in the east, and finally, the city of Arnhem was freed from Nazi power. The Germans surrendered their remaining hold on our country a few weeks later. This came just a few days before Germany fully surrendered to the Allied powers. For the people of the Netherlands, the war was over.

It took a long while for life to return to normal, of course. So much had been changed by the war. Some things would never be the same again.

I didn't like everything that happened after the Nazis retreated. Mrs. Van den Berg, the lady who'd given Hannah her tricycle, was among those paraded on the streets for being a Nazi sympathiser. She had had all of her hair shaved off her head, and her face had been painted bright orange. I don't know what happened to her after she was forced to walk around like this, but we never saw her again.

Our house escaped being searched by the Nazis, but my parents didn't regret building their secret attic room. It was a happy day when we took down the false roof, and refitted the original staircase to the upper room.

Hannah's bed was returned to its proper place, along with her china doll. She had slept through the entire war, unaware of the endless terrors and worries that we had suffered!

We returned the paintings and china ornaments that had been stored in the attic room to their proper places, making our home look bright and welcoming again, like it once had.

We hadn't heard from Jan since the food blockade had begun. My mother had tried sending him letters, but was never certain whether he received them. We knew that there had been a fierce battle between the Canadians and the SS in the centre of Groningen just a few weeks before the war ended, but we didn't know if Jan had been among those who'd been injured or killed amidst the gunfire.

I can still remember seeing my mother's face when that cheeky brother of mine knocked on our door, just before the first Christmas after the war had ended. Almost as though he'd never been away, when my mother started to open the door, he simply peered around its edge, smiled, and in a nonchalant way enquired, "Is anyone at home?" We all took turns to hug him like we'd never hugged anyone before.

Jan explained that he'd wanted to visit us many times, but leaving the factory was forbidden. He had had to move house several times, and he'd become increasingly concerned that his letters might be being intercepted, because several of the students at his university were thought to be members of the Dutch resistance.

He knew that he couldn't write to his little sister either, which would risk alerting the interest of the authorities in the family home. So, he felt that he had no option other than to wait until the time seemed right to make contact again.

Jan's arrival could not have been better timed. We were making plans for a special celebration at Christmas, the first that we'd had in many years. Mother had been saving flour to bake a special cake, and we'd even managed to lay our hands on a goose, which was going to provide our eagerly awaited supper. We'd already exchanged our simple, makeshift presents on St. Nicholas Day, but had chosen to wait until Christmas Day to share our special meal.

After Jan exchanged kisses and hugs with all of us, he wasted no time in visiting his little sister. I watched as he crouched beside her bed, clasping her hand in his two gentle palms, then kissing her gently on the forehead.

"Hello, little sister," he gently whispered. "I never stopped thinking of you, I promise! Big Jan loves Little Hannah!"

He kept hold of her hand, sitting quietly and wondering at her adorable face.

"You can hear me, my darling sister," he continued, "I know you can!"

At that moment, I swear that I saw Hannah desperately trying to break a smile. Astonished at what I saw, I found myself momentarily staring into space, unsure whether what I thought my senses were showing me was real. In a brief, hazy moment, the memory of the spinning wheel of Hannah's broken bike came rushing back to my mind.

Slowly, Hannah started to open her mouth, wanting to say something. Jan said that he felt her hand reaching for closer contact with his. We both saw her head twitch, as though she was trying to look toward us. These tiny movements gave us great joy, but Hannah was still a long way from waking from her very long sleep.

I bounded down the staircase as quickly as I could, screeching with excitement at my mother, who was working in the kitchen. "She's awake! She's awake! Hannah's awake!" I screamed.

My mother crossed both of her hands over her heart, and bowed her head. Falling to the ground, she burst into tears. Admittedly, I was surprised that she reacted this way, but I could soon see that hers were tears of joy, and I bent down to embrace her.

On Father's advice, we decided that we should let Hannah continue to rest as much as possible, until she was ready to fully come back to us. Jan spent much time with her alone, holding her hand, and telling her that he loved her.

Christmas Eve arrived, and Mother set to work, plucking the goose and laying out her baking trays.

We decided that after we returned from church, we would join together to sing a carol for Hannah. We surrounded her bed, held hands, and–breathing deeply–started our singing of *Stille Nacht*, the carol that we knew so well.

As we sang, we felt the love that bound us growing stronger. It almost felt as though we were all of the same body.

We continued singing the words of the third verse:
Silent night, Holy night,
Son of God, O how laughs
Love from your divine mouth,
Now the dawn of redeeming touches our hearts.

As we finished the fourth line, the miracle that we'd long been praying for, and then wished for in our hearts more than we'd ever done before, came true. Hannah opened her eyes and broke into a gentle smile.

We four brothers and our parents smiled back, reflecting the pure light that was shining on our faces. I had never felt so enraptured by a single moment.

And so, our Christmas Day came to be the best ever. Hannah took time to wake up fully, but before long, she was speaking and laughing with us, asking us questions about everything that had happened. Somehow, when I recounted all that we'd been through during those past six years or so, I wondered whether she might have been in a better place all along.

Afterword

The Sleeping Beauty is an enchanting tale, full of magic, and happening in a seemingly perfect world in which time literally can stand still.

The story begins with the yearning of a mother and father for a child. The baby that is then delivered comes as a precious gift, and she enthrals all who meet her. We are not told that the king and queen lust after the riches of their kingdom, only that they wish for the safety and happiness of their daughter. They are anxious to share their joy, inviting as many as they can to the celebratory feast, although this doesn't provide for the thirteenth wise woman, who then curses their daughter.

From the outset then, the focus of the story is on the things that matter most–love, kinship, and virtue. These we might find within ourselves, not in the material world.

The twelve that come to pay homage to the new princess offer gifts that will serve her well in her later life. She is destined to lead a virtuous life, to live a life of value, and to grow in beauty.

While the story points to the physical beauty of the princess, which grows as she matures, we might assume that we're meant to see that characteristics such as virtue, modesty, and humility are of equal if not

greater importance in creating what should be regarded as being beautiful.

The great hope and joy that enlivens the royal
household as the wise women present their gifts is
rudely interrupted by the unexpected arrival of the one
who has been excluded from the banquet. Her curse
not only spoils the party, but brings the harmonious
and expectant mood of the time to an abrupt close.

The king is unable to foresee how the wicked woman will be able to trick his daughter, perhaps believing that, through his actions, he might be able to alter
her fate. But he and his queen take their eyes off the
ball right at the moment when they should be watching
over their daughter most, and it is a simple curiosity
that leads the princess to find the old woman and her
spindle.

The hundred-year period of rest has been interpreted in various ways by different commentators. For
some, the long sleep represents the return of the souls
of those who are sleeping to a heavenly place–to their
true selves–a place where they are removed from the
illusion of the life of the material world. It's in a deep
sleep, according to this interpretation, that we connect
with our innermost selves. This is where we remember
who we are and come face-to-face with what is true. In
the mystical or heavenly realm, time has no meaning.

In an alternative search for meaning in the story,
the long period of rest speaks of a time when beauty

has been lost, an allegory of the Fall that separated mankind from the Divine. The worthy gifts that had been bestowed upon the princess are no longer present, and all appreciation of beauty is gone. The subjects of the kingdom who live beyond the castle walls and perimeter of the thorn bush lose hope of recovering the happiness that was once theirs. Sustaining lives of drudgery and hopelessness, they even start to forget the joy that had once prevailed in the land.

Taking a further reading of the story, the deep sleep alludes to the inner awakening of mortality and sexual maturity that's discovered during adolescence. The old woman's spinning wheel keeps turning, just as time keeps moving on. The princess is excited and fascinated by something new that she discovers–the spindle, or perhaps more appropriately, sexual attraction. This too is an encounter in a hidden room of the castle tower that's beyond her parents' glance.

These differing perspectives of what is happening don't contradict each other, of course. The experience of the royal household is one that we might all want to embrace, if we can find a way through the dense tangles of the thorn bushes that stand in our way.

If not for finding our true selves, this too is a journey worth taking for restoring beauty into our lives. Beauty matters because it stirs our souls and inspires; beauty gives hope, and brings an appreciation of the joy of being alive. By becoming beautiful–adopting the qualities of graciousness, gratitude, and other attributes that were gifted to the princess–we can walk through the thicket without hindrance.

The young men who first try to break through the thorn bush quickly falter in their efforts. A few who still remember what awaits them on the other side of the bush wait to see if they might learn from the experiences of those who attempt to cross it first, but still rush straight into the hedge before they are properly ready. All efforts to reach the heavily protected but nearby target are thwarted.

It's only when the time is right that a foreign prince arrives to make his attempt to reach the castle. He is freely allowed through the bush, being gifted an opening that he had done nothing by his own efforts to earn. But the time is right, and when the princess is awoken, the prince's very presence is enough to melt her heart.

Both the princess and prince know instinctively that they have found true love in the arms of each other, even though they have never met before. Their trust is placed in the knowing flame that burns within them, bringing them to meeting the one that they have unknowingly been yearning for for a long time.

The story ends as it began–offering hope, and with harmony restored in the kingdom. The bride and bridegroom are brought together, and the colourful life of the court returns once more.

THE SECOND TALE–CHAPTER ONE

Sinbad the porter and the second voyage of Sinbad the sailor

My name is Sinbad. I am a poor porter. I bear heavy burdens on my back, but I have not a sheqel to my name.

This past day I became acquainted with a most curious gentleman. I had found myself a good shelter where I might lay my bed, underneath the castellated walls of this man's splendid mansion.

This man's servants had called me to their master after he had heard me reciting a poem that had pleased him. I was greeted in the banqueting hall of his bejewelled palace, where he related a fantastic story about how a miraculous sea journey had helped him come upon his fortune.

I reasoned that this is a world so unjust; one in which a rich man like he can live in such luxury, while I must beg for my day's meal.

The man—whose name, strange to behold, was the same as mine—had invited me a second time to hear another of his adventures. And so once more, I found myself being taken past the sunken pool of his court-yard atrium, under a grand archway that led into a long, marble-tiled passageway, and finally to a finely polished acacia table, which stretched the full length of the banqueting hall.

"Welcome again, dear Sinbad," he began. "We share our name, but I tell you truthfully, that we are more than brothers." He chuckled to himself, sure that he spoke the truth. "My stories might seem to be strange to you, and my home may be filled with un-dreamed-of treasures, but I tell you truly, that my ex-perience can also be yours."

I didn't know what he meant, and I was yet unsure whether his stories were really true or just preposter-ous fantasies. But I enjoyed hearing a good story, and welcomed the succulent dishes that were laid before me, the likes of which I'd never tasted before.

After some time, my host began his story of a sec-ond voyage that he'd embarked on, telling of his travels to exotic islands that few men had set eyes upon before.

I listened intently, and now relate to you the same story that he spoke to me.

৯৯৯

"Following my first voyage, I had acquired riches beyond my wildest dreams. I bought the finest carpets, and filled my chests with clothes that would make a sultan proud. My servants prepared my meals and brought me the most charming wines. But after a while, I wearied of my habitual lifestyle and yearned again to go to sea.

And so, I left my house in the care of my servants, and travelled south to the great port of Basrah, where I'd once lived for a while. Here, I quickly came upon a group of merchants who were readying their ship for a voyage of many months. They took kindly to me, and after I had explained my business, I was pleased to accept their invitation to join their company.

We set sail on the next high tide, and soon were setting course for islands and distant harbours that were unknown to me. We traded well, exchanging goods with the townsfolk whose ports we visited, quickly making a handsome profit.

One day, we lay anchor off one of the most beautiful islands that I'd ever seen–a sanctuary seemingly devoid of man and beast. Along with others among our company, I ventured ashore to explore this enticing paradise.

While others gathered fruits, or cut virgin paths into the island's interior, I decided to rest myself under the shade of two giant trees, whose canopy would quite easily have provided shelter for all of the ship's company.

I ate some of the food that I had brought with me from the ship, and drank from the bottle of wine that I also kept with me. Before too long, I found myself drifting into a beautiful, deep sleep.

I don't know how long I may have been sleeping, but when I awoke, I saw that the ship was no longer at anchor. To my horror, I quickly realized that it had travelled far beyond the horizon.

I fell to my knees, pounding the sandy beach with my arms, crying out to Allah, "Why have I been so foolish to leave behind the great comforts that were mine in Baghdad?" I berated myself perhaps a hundred times, but it was to no avail. The ship was gone.

Eventually, I reasoned to myself that it must be because of Allah's Will that I found myself in my perplexing situation, and I called upon His help to lead me to a way of salvation. I did not know what to do, but decided that it might profit me to survey the island, to see if I might discover something that might assist me.

I scaled one of the two tall trees under which I'd rested. From my lofty position, I could see far around, in all directions. Nothing but sea and sky lay ahead of me, but at some distance inland, close to what I imagined was the centre of the island, I espied what looked like a gleaming white dome–the kind that might adorn a sultan's palace. I gathered the few remaining provisions that I had brought with me from the ship in my leather bag, and set off toward this strange structure.

It took me many hours to reach the shining edifice that I'd seen, where I quickly started exploring the strange building, looking for a door through which I might be able to request entry.

But to my despair, there was no door to be found– the whole structure was perfectly round. As I clambered over its slippery walls, I learned that it would not easily give up its secret.

By now, the sun was beginning to journey low toward the nether regions, and I began to search for a place where I might rest my head for that night.

Suddenly, the sky became overcast with a dark shadow. I feared that a great storm might soon rip across the island. But no sooner had I run for cover, than I realized that what I had thought was a cloud was in fact a gigantic bird, the like of which I had never seen before.

It was then that I suddenly remembered hearing tales of such a mysterious creature, a bird known as a roc, which was said to dwell on its own beautiful island. I had thought such tales to be mere fantasy, but now I could see for myself that they were true.

The roc alighted on the dome, which I now understood to be her egg. While I could still glimpse a little light, I made quickly for one of her giant legs, whose perimeter was as broad and as strong as the trunk of a giant cedar tree.

Against the vast expanse of her mighty body, the roc did not notice me, and thus I had no trouble securing myself with my turban to the stem of her leg. I reasoned that Allah had brought me here, and that His rescuing might be found in my being carried far away by this most awesome of creatures.

At daybreak, my hope was satisfied, as the roc took leave of her egg and lifted herself high into the heavens.

Soon, I could see the whole earth laid out before me. We travelled at such speed that I could barely keep hold of my senses. But the bird's flight was smooth, and my anchoring felt secure.

After a while, I saw another island coming into view. The roc dived at great speed toward it, and as she made landfall, I quickly untied myself from her giant limb.

No sooner was I free than I noticed the prey that she had set upon—a giant serpent, that was now being carried high in her grasp back to the island that we had departed only a little earlier.

I had never seen a serpent of such size, but it must have appeared small to her. I watched her soar high above me, before I proceeded to investigate the new land that I had been brought to.

I was astonished to see that all around me were diamonds of the most extraordinary quality and size. Never before had I encountered any stones of such dazzling beauty. I felt excited by my discovery, but my joy quickly turned to great fear when I saw that there were several serpents ahead of me, larger and more monstrous than the one that had been carried away by the roc.

I looked around for a possible path that might allow me to flee to safety, but save for the sea, I was surrounded on all sides by the steepest and tallest of all mountains.

I beat my breast and scolded myself for being so unfortunate to have exchanged a beautiful island for this one. How could I possibly escape this most terrible of places?

In terror, I scurried into a cave, filling its entrance with as many large rocks as I could, praying that this might afford me some safety from the serpents outside.

In my desperation to find sanctuary from the terrifying reptiles, I hadn't noticed that I was not alone inside the cave. One of the giant serpents was coiled up in a corner, protecting her eggs. For now, it appeared that she hadn't noticed me, but I was so overcome with fear, that I could do nothing but shudder.

When night fell, I heard the hissing of many serpents outside, which gave me no peace, nor release from my terror. I did not sleep a wink that night, but was happy that the brooding creature that I'd shared the night with hadn't been disturbed by my presence.

At daybreak, I quietly cleared the rocks that I'd used to block the entrance to the cave, and slipped away as quietly as I could. It seemed that most of the serpents had gone now. I assumed that they were sheltering in their dens, lest they attract the attention of the roc when she returned to seek out her next meal.

I was so exhausted, that after walking only a short way, I collapsed onto the ground, and was soon sleeping deeply.

No sooner had I fallen asleep, then I was awoken by a loud noise close by—a sound not unlike the crack of a whip on a criminal's back. The sharp sound startled me, but I was even more astonished to discover that it was made by a large piece of raw meat that had fallen from the sky, as it had caught on to the pointed edges of one of the diamonds in front of me.

Soon I saw more pieces of meat falling into the valley, each landing squarely on top of a diamond.

Then it came to me in a flash! I recalled an old mariner's tale about merchants who mined diamonds from an impenetrable valley on some hostile island. Their method was to catapult pieces of meat onto the diamonds from a lofty position that they were able to access from the other side of the island.

Once attached to a diamond, the meat attracted the attention of eagles that roosted close to where the merchants were hiding. The birds dived into the valley to plunder the meat, carrying the attached diamonds back with them to their nests.

This is when the merchants would pounce, making a great noise and charging at the birds to scare them away. And so, the merchants were able to lay their hands on the precious jewels without needing to brave a descent into the valley.

I quickly resolved a plan that, with Allah's help, might allow me to escape my awful situation.

Firstly, I searched for the most appealing diamonds that I could find, gathering as many as I could into my leather bag, which was now emptied of my provisions.

I then hunted for the choicest piece of meat that had fallen nearby. Again unravelling my turban, I securely fastened the large piece of meat onto my back, and then lay facedown, holding myself as still as I could between the diamonds.

No sooner had I adopted this position, than an eagle swooped low above me, fastening her claws on the precious meat cargo that was strapped to my back. I was carried away by the eagle along with the meat, being taken high above the ground by the great winged creature.

"May Allah be praised!" I felt my heart singing. But I hadn't yet finished my adventure.

As I'd expected, once the bird had landed, a merchant soon arrived to scare it away. I had quickly loosened myself from the meat, and crouched against the wall of the precipice that the bird had chosen for its nest.

The merchant was surprised to see me with the diamond when I emerged from my hiding place, but did not give me a civil greeting.

"Why have you stolen our diamond?" he angrily demanded.

"I beg you, sir, to speak to me more kindly when you know that I selected this diamond with my own hands. And I have many more, plenty for you and your companions, if you will allow me to share your passage away from here."

The merchant begrudgingly agreed to take me to his camp, where I related my story to his fellow travellers. They were astonished, but when I begged the man who had found me to take his pick of the diamonds that I had gathered, he and his company were soon won over to my advantage.

Content that he might never need to put sail again for the riches that just one of these diamonds would buy, he accepted the smallest of my offering, and I was pleased to offer still others to his companions.

Satisfied that they need continue their mission no longer, we abandoned the camp and started on our treacherous journey back to the ship, taking two full days to get there.

We drew in the anchor and sailed for other islands and isolated parts of the continent, where we were able to make a good trade from the commodities that we exchanged.

On one island that we happened upon, we collected the fragrant juice that is known as camphire, which exudes from a hole bored into a type of tree that grows there.

On that island too, I saw the creature that we call the rhinoceros—a beast not quite the size of an elephant, but well able to do battle with such an animal, using its sharp horn as a spear to blind its adversary.

To our good fortune, we did not cross paths with a rhinoceros, but after gathering our quarry, quickly set sail for another land of rich pickings.

We came at last to Basrah, where I resolved never to set to sea again.

The merchants were able to sell their diamonds at a great profit, and I set off on my journey home to Baghdad. Just one of my diamonds sold in the souk near here for almost ten times the wealth that I had gained from my first voyage."

෭ၴ

My host finished his story here, offering me a whole sheqel as a gift, as he had the night earlier, before inviting me to join him again the following evening to hear yet another incredible tale.

But for me to say more of that, my dear friends, must wait for another time.

The two Sarahs

Sarah and I had been friends since we met in High School. We'd been through college together–she taking a course in media studies, and me earning my degree in business administration. Having left college last year, we were sharing an apartment together, though our lives only occasionally coincided.

Neither of us had been able to get proper work since we'd graduated. We'd both had odd jobs here and there, cleaning offices and serving hamburgers, but these had rarely lasted more than a few weeks at a time, and hardly paid the rent.

For that, we were largely dependent on Sarah's parents, who seemed to never quarrel when she asked them for another loan. They weren't exactly hard up, mind you, owning an electronics business, which had done very well during the dot com boom.

Sarah was their only child, and they still treated her as though she was in her early teens. Despite her half-hearted attempts to hold down a job, I think that she knew that her folks would make sure that she would never be left wanting.

During the time that I'd known her, they'd bought her a glitzy new Fiat 500, gave her a twenty-four karat gold necklace when she managed to just scrape her way through college, and, she tells me, settled all her debts after taking that pointless course.

My parents could not compete with hers, and I doubt that they would ever want to. My father works every hour that God sends fixing old cars, while, when asked, my mother simply describes her job as being in the "retail profession". They try to support me as best they can, but their means have never stretched to laying out on brand-new Fiat 500's and expensive jewellery.

In case of possible confusion, I should perhaps explain before going any further that I too am called Sarah. When we are together, our friends call us "Big Sarah" and "Little Sarah"–me being the taller of the two. I suppose Sarah is a common enough name, but having two Sarahs in one house creates confusion at times, when we pick up on our answerphone messages.

Little Sarah–or "Sis", as I usually call her–was increasingly getting on my nerves. I didn't object to her late nights out and long lie-in's–that was her business. What did get me down was her refusal to do virtually anything around the house. Dishes were left unwashed, clothes sprawled over the back of the sofa, and the bath was always left to soak up a puddle of hairs whenever she took a shower.

It was nearly always me who ended up doing the cleaning. Whenever I complained, she suggested that we get a cleaner in to do the job, seemingly forgetting that cleaners cost money, and that is something that I at least don't have.

To be honest, it was comical watching her whenever she did make a vague attempt at cleaning up. She always managed to drop a glass or break a plate when washing up, and once I saw her kicking and screaming at the vacuum, because it wasn't picking up dust quite as effortlessly as she'd expected. Of course, the dust bag was full, as any old fool would know.

While I loved her dearly, I resented her too. She didn't seem to have any sense of shared responsibility, and spent her days in what seemed to me to be a total dream world.

My time was mainly spent trying to find a decent job. I'd worked hard at college, rarely showing my face in the union bar, and becoming something of a permanent fixture in the library. I wanted to do well in my exams, and was told by my tutor that I'd only narrowly missed out on getting a first.

You'd think that the world would be crying out for someone with a good business administration degree, but I learned long ago that any hope that I might once have had of just waltzing into a job was naive fantasy. I knew that I had the skills that the big employers wanted, but for some unknown reason, they kept passing me by.

I kept putting together applications, of course. Over the past year, I'd sent my resume to maybe a hundred or more agencies, and responded to one hundred more job advertisements.

But the interviews were few, and the competition was always supposedly superior to me. "Thank you for your very impressive application Miss Prior," began the typical rejection letter. "While you appear to have excellent skills, we have received applications from an exceptionally large number of very high calibre candidates, whose qualifications more closely meet our needs. We are very sorry on this occasion that we can't consider you for interview, and wish you well in your continued search for a suitable position."

It was all bullshit of course, but in an employers' market, I was in no position to argue.

The letters did start to really get me down. That's if I got a reply at all, which more often than not wasn't the case. I reasoned to myself that it was just a matter of time before the right job came along, and determined to keep working away at my applications.

Of course, writing applications wasn't a regular part of my housemate's routine. She was convinced that it wouldn't be long before record producers would be fighting each other to secure her signature on a gold-plated contract. My dear little sis was convinced that she was going to be a star–not that she'd even started singing until she had an idea that it would be fun to join a band while at college.

As far as I was concerned, she barely had a musical note in her. But she didn't see things that way. Take, for example, one Tuesday evening a few months ago.

"Are you coming down *The Blue Moon* later tonight?" she quizzed me, as I was attempting to scrape the fat from the frying pan that she'd left sitting on the gas hob. "It's an open mike night tonight, and I'm planning to set the place alight with a new little number that I've been working on!"

"I can't Sweetie, I'm sorry," I replied. "I've got an application to finish. It's the deadline for submissions tomorrow."

"Can't you give it a break for once, Big Sis?" she teased, "I've told you many times that you should try and chill out more, but you never listen to my advice."

I had to be honest that once in a while I would like to get out and enjoy myself, but money was tight, and I was determined to get myself a job before I let myself indulge in too many frivolous adventures.

"We've been over this many times before," I reminded her. "You know that I'd love to come, but I've got to get myself sorted."

Sarah knew that this was a conversation that wasn't worth pursuing. We'd rarely come to blows over our differing views on life, but privately resented something of what each other had. I suppose that that's why we'd stayed as good friends, dysfunctional though our relationship may have been.

Sarah disappeared out of the house a little after eight, and I didn't see her again until later the next morning. There was nothing unusual about this–I was usually up busying myself with something soon after sunrise, whereas Sarah rarely made it to her bed before two or three in the morning.

The application that I'd been anxious to finish was in vain. I had high hopes that that one might have led to something, but it took no more than a few days for the familiar "sorry, but no" response to come through.

Sarah's night had gone considerably better than mine, it seems. At least, that's what she told me the day after. We usually shared meals together, which gave Sarah the perfect opportunity to sound out on whatever latest wild adventure she'd just experienced, not to mention the countless elaborate stories that she recounted about her past.

She'd done a lot of travelling. When she was younger, her parents had taken her on cruises, safaris in the Serengeti, and scuba diving on the Great Barrier Reef. Somehow, she'd always encountered amazing characters during her journeys, and claimed to have found herself in quite a few tight spots too. But of course, she always came through unscathed, and seemingly better off for her many adventures.

"It was a fab night last night!" she started, as we bit into our chilli, which I'd prepared for our lunch. "I was last up on stage, and the crowd just loved me! They were shouting and calling for more when I finished my set, and the house band was just brilliant!"

I tried to feign interest, not wishing to discourage her. "Sounds fab!" I replied, trying to sound as enthusiastic as I could. "What numbers did you sing in the end?"

She proceeded to elaborate on the details of her performance, taking special care to remark on the audience's reception.

"What's really cool is that I found out that auditions are going on in town next week for some new TV show involving budding musicians! Apparently, the producers are looking to sign up a new band and then follow their progress as they prepare for the big time. This is my big opportunity, Sis! I told you that it would only be a matter of time!"

"That's fantastic news!" I lied. "What a brilliant opportunity!"

She proceeded to detail the lifestyle that she felt destined for, while attempting to assure me that nothing would change in our friendship when she'd made it onto the big stage.

For the days that followed, she barely seemed to think about anything else. "What look do you think is going to impress them best at the audition?" she asked me, flitting in and out of her room as she changed into a series of different costumes.

"I love the torn jeans and studded black leather jacket," I offered, "But it's your white chiffon dress that really brings out the true goddess in you! You need to show them more than just the everyday girl look."

"You're so right," she agreed, "That dress really feels like it was made for a true diva like me! My glowing radiance cannot help but shine through!"

I didn't really have much of a sense about fashion, preferring to choose clothes that were as comfortable and practical as possible. Sarah never could decide what to wear, and whenever we were out together in town, was always hunting for something new on the clothes racks of one premium boutique or another.

She booked an appointment with the hairdresser for the morning of her audition, and had started to debate what jewellery she should wear–something that would be fit for a star, but not outshine her startling personality.

I hesitated to ask which songs she'd chosen for her ten-minute appearance in front of the producers, not to mention the small matter of how she was getting on with rehearsals.

"Everything in good time, Sweetie!" She chuckled. "Star quality is what those guys are looking for, and I've got more of that than they'll know how to handle!"

It seems that she'd chosen to sing the same song that had supposedly wowed the crowd at *The Blue Moon*. "At least she knows the words," I mused to myself.

The day of the audition arrived all too quickly, and I wished her every success as she set off for her meeting with destiny. "Break a leg!" was all she said, as she blew me a kiss and headed off into the daylight with her suit bag.

I have to admit that she looked the part. The hairdresser had braided her hair in a style that might have been worn by a Greek goddess. I did feel a little jealous of her, if not also wanting her to do well. She was my closest buddy, after all.

Who was to say that she might really shine with the producers, and might soon be gracing the TV screens of the nation, being stalked by an adoring fan base and a gaggle of paparazzi, with their ever-flashing cameras?

She'd spoken about what she was sure would happen. I could see that she would step into a celebrity lifestyle very easily. The stretched limos, the awards receptions, the appearances on TV chat shows–she'd take it all in her stride. The life that she'd long claimed was due to her now seemed but a hair's breadth from her grasp.

I cleaned the house, and set out a small table with a couple of glasses and a bottle of sparkling wine, ready to crack open to celebrate her successful audition. I even hastily put together a paper banner, plastering a welcome home message on the hallway door–"Well done, Little Sis! You're my superstar!"

Sarah arrived home a little after five. She was still wearing her chiffon dress and stunning necklace, but her demeanour marked her out as a crestfallen angel, a person dejected.

"I'm so sorry, darling," I quietly tried to console her, guiding her toward the couch. "Come, let's sit down, and you can tell me all about it."

"Those morons!" she screamed, "Can't they see real talent, even when it's right in front of their eyes!" The first of a steady stream of tears began to flow down her cheek. "I gave it my all, but those fucking bastards just don't get it! They just don't get it!" I placed my arm around her shoulder, letting her know that I felt her pain. "They said that I needed to work on my voice, for fuck's sake! Can't they see that I know how to fucking sing!"

I'd rarely seen Sarah feeling so angry. She didn't easily allow herself to cry, at least not in front of others.

I decided that there would be a better time to suggest that the producers might have been concerned with how well she could sing, as much as how well she might look the part for the role. This was not the moment for such analysis.

Sarah rested her head on my shoulder, and I tightened my embrace on her. We sat in silence for quite some time, trying to make sense of what had happened.

This was to be the first of a number of evenings that we spent together sharing in heart-to-heart conversation, just like we used to do.

As we opened up, it came to me that perhaps we might be able to help each other.

Sarah might be able to help me snap out of the angry moods that were now beginning to take a hold on me, as I tried to let out my feelings stirred by all those wretched rejection letters.

I realised that I needed to save myself before I might withdraw into a bitter shell. Perhaps it was time for me to join Sarah on one or two of her nightly outings downtown?

I could see too, all too painfully, that Sarah needed my support. The experience of the audition had hit her hard. I don't think that she'd faced rejection like that before, and this episode was all the more painful for the hope that she'd placed in it.

If I lacked good fashion sense and was not the life and soul of the party, at least I might be able to help my friend face up to reality. Maybe together we could find some practical way of sorting out our disappointing lives.

Sarah was fully on board with my suggestion that we work together toward realizing the plans that we had. She started to spend more time indoors, and even showed a readiness to keep the place tidy.

In turn, she introduced me to her favourite bars, where she seemed to know everybody. I felt better for these occasional sorties into a world of tequila shots and spaced-out music. I felt my spirit lifting, and my whole manner changing.

Sarah helped me see that my effort with applications hadn't all been in vain. She pointed out that I'd made it through to second interviews a number of times, and, like her, must only have been passed over for selection at the very last hurdle.

Her words gave me hope to keep trying. But it was my changing feelings that helped me most. I began to feel more confident, more positive, and more alive.

This must have played a part when I was offered my next interview. I immediately gelled with the interviewer, and it came as little surprise when I was invited for a further interview. I was told that I was on a short-list of twelve, which was not uncommon at that stage. But I obviously created a strong impression. This time it was I who received the offer letter.

I managed to find a time to broach the subject of Sarah's singing voice, explaining to her that I hadn't wanted to hurt her feelings or spoil her fun by mentioning this before. I didn't feel that she would have been able to take my criticism well if I had.

But now that she'd begun to reflect more philosophically on her recent experience, she was able to accept that there was room for improvement in training her voice. She has recently embarked on a course of lessons with a singing coach, and is hoping to get back in front of the open mike before too long. There will be other opportunities for her to shine in the fullness of time, I'm sure.

I've also been helping Sarah to start thinking properly about getting a job. I've helped her put together a number of applications for media positions, and she's already been offered a number of interviews. I don't think that she'll need much advice from me on her interview style, now that her confidence is returning and she sees that there are new possibilities opening up to her.

We make a great team. Even though we're just good friends, we know how to bring out the best in each other. I'm certain that we're now both heading

along a steady path that will bring happiness into our
lives.

Afterword

The Second Voyage of Sinbad the Sailor is perhaps the
best known of the seven which form part of the much
larger canon of the tales of the *One Thousand and One
Arabian Nights*, the fantastical collection of stories
that Scheherazade related to the Shahryār (or Sultan),
in her quest to be spared the fate that had befallen
many women before her[5].

---

[5] The frame story for *The One Thousand and One
Arabian Nights* tells that the sultan felt so angered
when he discovered that his first wife had betrayed
him, that he resolved never to allow another woman to
be unfaithful to him. Instead, he married a new virgin
every night, and then beheaded her the following day.
Eventually, Scheherazade offered herself to spend a
night with Shahryār. She relates a remarkable story
that fully enthralls him, but leaves the tale unfinished
and begging a tantalizing ending. The enthralled sultan so enjoys the story that he permits Scheherazade
one further night to conclude the tale. But Scheherazade continues the ruse, ultimately engaging the
king in storytelling for 1,001 nights, after which time
he is besotted with her.

Like all stories that form part of a greater whole, including *Jack and the Beanstalk, The Second Voyage of Sinbad the Sailor* may best be appreciated when taken in its full context. However, each of the seven voyages can also stand on its own.

The fact that both the porter and the old sailor bear the same name might give a clue to the fact that they are really the same person. One lives in sumptuous luxury, spending his days spinning yarns and finding pleasure in fantasy. The other sits just outside the mansion, where he grumbles endlessly about the rotten lot in life that he's been dealt, while he still manages to navigate the day-to-day practicalities of living.

Both Sinbads gain advantage from their encounters. The sailor finds a reliable audience for bragging about his many adventures, as well as possibly a muse for creating them; the porter is served a decent meal each night, and even earns a monetary reward that well compensates him for his troubles.

Sinbad the sailor lives for pleasure and adventure. Sinbad the porter lives in the real world–a world in which every day he faces a struggle to survive.

The sailor can't let go of his need for dangerous adventures even when he has gained much, yearning to put to sea again. Perhaps it is his carnal nature that motivates his lust for discovering any new thing that might satisfy his senses; perhaps a curiosity driven by a wild imagination. Either way, he ignores any risks that might stand in his way, only recognising that he may have stretched himself too far when he encounters peril after peril.

The recounting of the sailor's stories provides an escape from the drudgery of the porter's everyday life. Significantly, it's after darkness falls that the stories are related–the time that's usually reserved for sleeping and dreaming. In the dreams of the sailor–that are really also *his* dreams–the porter can see possibilities that might allow him to move beyond his current station and achieve wonderful things, but possibly too, ones that might require him to come face-to-face with danger.

The sailor knows that he must return to reality at some point, and he acknowledges as much to the porter–both with his words, and by offering him a gift during each of his visits.

The story's presentation of two characters allows each to project something of his inner self onto the other. The sailor projects the part of his shadow that begrudges the greatness that he sees in the life of the sailor, but the sailor responds by observing that there's a higher self in his brother.

Often what we project reveals something about ourselves, both the good and the bad that we repress. This is perhaps why we can learn so much about ourselves through our interaction with others, if only we might allow ourselves to turn inward when we notice ourselves judging those who are close to us, not to mention the strangers that we meet too.

Ultimately, both personalities in the story have their merits, and both need to complement each other if Sinbad, or any person, is to achieve ultimate happiness and wholeness. A starting point on this journey is to recognize that there are discordant aspects of our psyche, and that one—unimaginative attachment to reality on the one hand, or constant gratification-seeking from flights of fantasy on the other—may tend to dominate in our approach to life.

This is a struggle that we all have to wrestle with.

The three little pigs

There was a time long ago when monkeys chewed tobacco, and pigs spoke in rhyme.

This is the story of three of such little pigs, and the varied fortunes that awaited them when they set off to find their way in the world.

The eldest of the pigs was very lazy. He rarely helped his mother and brothers around the house, and loved nothing more than to spend all of his time wallowing in mud. Nothing pleased him more than a rainy day, when the mud was especially thick and sticky!

"My son," his mother so often desperately pleaded, "You never care for bringing all of your mud into our house, and your belly is always dirty. How I wonder how you will get on when you are older! One day, you'll be sorry that you didn't listen to your poor old mother!"

The next eldest pig didn't enjoy wallowing in mud, keeping himself clean, but he was very greedy. When it was feeding time, he would always push and shove his way to fight for the biggest portion and the best food in the trough, not caring that his brothers and mother might starve.

"Oh my dear son," said his mother, "Your greediness will lead you into trouble when you are older! You never listen to the advice of your poor old mother!"

The youngest pig was the cleverest of the three. He listened well to his mother's advice, and always worked hard around the house. He didn't like playing in the mud, and was always the last to take his turn at the trough at mealtimes.

The pigs lived happily together for a time, but the poor old sow was getting very weak and unable to care for her young ones.

"I am very weak," she told the three little pigs one day, "And soon I will be here no longer. My dear children, now you must make your own way in the world. Go with my blessing, and make your own homes."

And so, the three little pigs wished their mother well, promising to visit her often, and set off on their separate ways.

The eldest pig thought to himself that he would not spend much time making his house. "Time is too short for building houses when there's lots of playing to be done!" he reasoned.

Soon, he came across a man who was carrying a large bale of straw.

"Hello, kind sir," began the pig, "Might I take some straw from you in order to build myself a house?"

"It would be a pleasure!" replied the man, and he sorted out a generous quantity of straw to give to the pig.

The pig thanked the man, and then set about building his house. It didn't take him long to finish, because the straw was very light and long, quickly forming walls and a roof for his tiny house.

The pig was very pleased with himself, and soon set about his usual task of rolling around in the mud.

Later that day, after a long and tiring time of playing outside, the little pig went back into his house to rest.

Not long after, a wolf passed by and, seeing the little straw house, thought to himself, "I wonder who lives there?"

The wolf knocked on the door. "May I come in?" he asked, waiting for a reply.

"But I don't know who you are!" answered the pig, "And I'm very tired after my long day."

The wolf asked again if he might be allowed in, but the pig sternly replied, "No, not by the hair of my chiny chin chin!"

The wolf was very angry at this, and he growled back at the pig in an instant, "Well, if you won't open the door, I'll huff and I'll puff and I'll blow your house down!"

With all his strength, the wolf did huff and puff, and in no time at all, the poor little pig's house came tumbling down all around him. The wolf pounced on the little pig, and took him home to his den.

Meanwhile, the next eldest pig had set off on a different road. "I'll not waste time building my house," he mused, "There's too little time before my dinner."

A short way along the path, the little pig met a man who was carrying a large bundle of sticks.

"Good morning, sir," said the pig, "Might you allow me to have some of your sticks, so that I might build myself a house that will be strong when the winds come, and keep me safe from the rain?"

"Why certainly, little pig!" answered the man, "Here, take what you need!"

The little pig was very grateful to the man, but took nearly all of the sticks that he'd gathered. He then quickly built his house, with the sticks taking very little time to plant into the ground.

"Well that was easy!" the little pig chuckled to himself. "Now I can set about making my dinner!"

Soon, the wolf came walking by and, noticing the little pig's new little house, wondered to himself, "Who might live in this house, which I've never seen before?"

The wolf knocked on the door of the house and said, "Please let me in, my dear friend!"

"But I don't know who you are!" replied the pig, "And I have nothing to offer you."

The wolf knocked again and demanded, "Let me in!"

But the little pig was sure that this wasn't someone who he should welcome into his house. "No, not by the hair of my chiny chin chin!" said the pig.

"Well, if you won't let me in," roared the wolf, "I'll huff and I'll puff and I'll blow your house down!"

And, true to his word, the wolf did huff and puff, and the pig's tiny house of sticks quickly came tumbling down. The wolf pounced on the pig, and took him home to his den.

While all of this was happening, the youngest pig had not gone far from his mother's house when he met a man who was selling bricks. "I must build myself a house that will be strong when the winds come, and keep me safe from the cunning wolf," he thought.

The little pig was very clever, and he remembered his mother's advice to keep himself safe. "The bricks will make my house strong," he thought to himself. And so he politely asked the man, "Kind sir, please will you allow me to have some of your bricks, so that I might build myself a house?"

The man was very happy to let the pig take some of his bricks, and the pig thanked him for his kindness.

It took the pig a long time to build his house. He thought about nothing else until he was finished. Finally, after a very long day, he crept into his house and bolted the door.

A short while later, the wolf came wandering by. "I've never seen that house before," he thought to himself. "I wonder who might live there?" And so, he knocked on the door of the house, and asked, "Please let me in!"

But the little pig realised that this might be a trick, and he wasn't quickly taken in by the wolf's cunning. "No sir, not now, for I have had a very long day and am too tired to speak with you."

The wolf again knocked on the door, this time speaking much more loudly, "Let me into your house!"

Realising that he was in danger, the little pig promptly replied, "No, not by the hair of my chiny chin chin!"

"Well, if you won't let me in, I'll huff and I'll puff and I'll blow your house down!" screamed the wolf, just as he had done when the other two brothers had not let him in.

The wolf huffed and puffed with all his might, and beat his hands against the walls of the little pig's house. But the house didn't shake an inch.

Exhausted, the wolf felt very angry that he'd been foiled, and set about a plan to trick the little pig.

"Little pig, may I tell you about a field that I saw earlier that's full of lovely ripe turnips?"

"Oh, yes please!" answered the pig, although realising that the wolf might be trying to trick him. "Where might we find this field?"

"At Mr. Smith's farm," replied the wolf. "Perhaps we might go there together, tomorrow at six?"

"Oh yes, that would be a fine idea!" answered the pig, and bade the wolf goodnight.

The pig did go to the turnip field the following morning, but he set off at five in order to be there long before the wolf arrived. He was already home when the wolf came to call for him.

"Are you ready to go and gather some fine turnips, my good friend?" asked the wolf, when he came by the little pig's house at six o'clock.

"Oh sir! " cried the pig through the small letterbox that he'd cut into his door, "I got up early this morning, and have already been to the field to collect my share!"

The wolf was angry that the pig would not join him, but devised another plan that might catch him out.

"Well, perhaps you might like to join me tomorrow to gather some apples?" suggested the wolf. "I know where there's a very large tree with lots of delicious apples just waiting to be picked!"

"Oh, that would be wonderful!" replied the pig. "Where did you find such a fine apple tree?"

"It's at Merry Garden," answered the wolf. "I'll call for you tomorrow morning at five, and we can go together."

The little pig realised that the wolf was again trying to trick him, and so when the next morning came, he rose at four o'clock in order to be at Merry Garden first.

The pig's journey took longer than he'd expected, and he had to scale the tree in order to pick the apples. To his great fright, while he was still perched on one of its branches, he saw the wolf approaching him.

"I'm sorry, Mr. Wolf," said the pig, "But the sun was already rising early this morning, and I thought that I would come quickly to fetch some apples."

The wolf was very angry that he'd been let down by the pig again, but could not see how he could pounce on the little pig where he was, because he was safe in the trees.

"Have you found many good apples?" asked the wolf.

"Oh yes, very many! Let me throw you one!" replied the pig, and he threw down the biggest and juiciest of the apples that he'd gathered.

While the wolf went off to fetch the apple, the little pig climbed down the tree and ran home to his house as quickly as he could, just managing to close the door before the wolf arrived behind him.

Now, the wolf was very angry, but he'd not yet given up trying to catch the pig.

"Did I mention that there's a fair in the town tomorrow?" asked the wolf.

"No sir, I don't remember you mentioning that," said the pig. "That sounds like something I should like to visit!"

"Well, perhaps we can go together tomorrow afternoon? I'll call by your house at three," offered the wolf.

"Yes, I would very much like to go!" replied the pig.

But as before, the pig knew that he must not be tricked by the wolf, and so he left an hour earlier than the time he was due to call by. At the fair, the pig bought a butter churn, but as he was making his way home, he saw the wolf approaching him from further down the hill.

The pig did not know what to do, and was very scared. Trying to think of a plan to save himself, he jumped inside the churn, and, rocking his body to and fro', managed to set the churn rolling down the hill.

The wolf was very scared when he saw this strange object rolling toward him, and he ran for the woods, desperate to hide.

Later, the wolf returned to the little pig's house to tell him the story of his frightening ordeal. "I was scared for my life!" said the wolf. "Never before had I seen such a thing racing toward me!"

"You fool!" laughed the pig. "It was me inside a butter churn that you saw. I hid in there so that you wouldn't find me!"

The wolf was angrier than he'd ever been before when he realised that he'd again been tricked. This time, there and then, he decided that he would catch the pig and take him home for his supper!

"Well, this time you won't escape me!" roared the wolf. "I'm going to climb onto your roof and drop down your chimney to eat you!"

The pig was very frightened at this, but being clever, he quickly made a plan to save himself from the wolf's terrible promise.

He quickly made a fire underneath the chimney, and placed a large cooking pot of water on top of it. When he heard the wolf making his way down the chimney, the little pig quickly removed the lid from the pot, and–in an instant–the wolf tumbled straight into the steaming water!

Quickly, the pig placed the lid back on the cooking pot, and soon the wolf was boiling over what was now a blazing fire.

The little pig ate healthily that evening, and then slept peacefully in his bed.

A game of three halves

They say that football is a game of two halves. Well, I can already go one better than that, having lived through what seems to me to have been three different lifetimes.

Life was fine until my mother got ill and had to move into a nursing home. She'd kept me fed and watered, and made sure that I never missed out on enjoying myself. I couldn't afford to pay the rent for the house alone, so I moved into a bedsit in Vauxhall and hunted around for a job.

That was back in the 80's, when jobs were much easier to come by than they are now. I dropped out of college and never got to go to uni, but that didn't stop me sorting out a nice little number for myself with an advertising agency.

For an eighteen-year-old, the job paid well, and the office was right in the centre of Soho—perfect for dropping in on my favourite watering holes on and off the Charing Cross Road.

I used to start off most nights at *The Round Table*, before moving on to *The Porcupine*, and then *The Jack Horner*. On Thursdays and Fridays, I usually ended up at The *Hippodrome*, or some other club around the back of Leicester Square.

Those were heady days. I had money in my pocket, and rarely had a care in the world. I used to drop in to see my old mum from time to time, but she was struggling to remember who I was most of the time. "Make sure you look after yourself...Get yourself a good job...Save up hard," was all that she'd ever say each time I saw her.

I liked to slip out for a jar at lunchtime, just to get away from the office for an hour or two. No one ever seemed concerned what time I got back, so long as the work got done. "Work hard, play hard," was the unofficial motto of Best & Partners.

Looking back, I can see that my contribution was more in the "play hard" arena, but I thought that I was doing my bit at the time.

I can't deny that I knew how to have a good time. At eighteen, you don't care too much about stashing your pennies away for some future that might never come. Living for the moment was what being in London was all about in 1985, and it was the perfect time to be young and single.

That said, I wasn't single for very long. I played around, of course. All those hormones racing through my body wouldn't let me do anything else. My girl was Sally, who I'd met at the office. Sally enjoyed a drink or two, and would come clubbing with me most Friday nights. But she took her career far more seriously than me, and refused to stay out late during the week.

It wasn't long before we were an item, and, cutting a long story short, were soon shacked up together.

Being with Sally was like being at home with my mum in the old days, only ten times better. I got my shirts ironed, my dinner put in front of me, and my breakfasts brought to me on a tray. This was usually when Sally shouted in my ear for me to get up, just as she was leaving for work. I nearly always had a hangover in the morning, and often didn't get to my desk until well after ten. No one ever seemed to give a damn.

What made Sally so special was her body–so soft, so many curves, so sexy. I just loved running my hands over her breasts, stroking her back, and letting her tongue become entangled with mine. She was a very sexual lady, and, like me, always hungry for natural, raw sex. Handcuffs, uniforms, blindfolds–we tried them all. We were having the time of our lives.

Looking back, I can't see what Sally saw in me. To be frank, I was a total arsehole, rarely doing anything for her, but still expecting her to wait on me hand and foot. She did that, of course, like making sure that I got up every morning, even if this did involve bellowing obscenities into my ear and beating me around the head with a pillow.

Sally often covered for me at work, making up all sorts of fanciful excuses for me when I didn't manage to struggle in to the office. My boss must have thought that he'd employed someone who was never far from death's door, being as prone to chronic diseases and permanent ailments as I supposedly was. But they didn't question me about my many days of absence, probably because Sally was good at her job, and they didn't want to take her to task over the lies that she created on my behalf.

Like most good things, my paradise lifestyle wasn't to last for long. The agency was just one of many firms that found themselves in hot water when the money-making bubble of the time burst. A sharp fall-off in new business led them to deciding that they needed to let a few of us go. I never knew why I was one of those selected for the chop, but my boss assured me that it had nothing to do with me personally.

Sally wasn't convinced that he was fully telling the truth. She berated my reckless lifestyle and poor regard for the company's time, certain that it was this that had marked me out as a man to be fired. She was right of course, but I didn't see things that way at the time.

I was quite happy not to have to face dragging myself out of bed every morning, and the extra few grand that I was given as my severance package was very handy for paying off some of the debts that I'd accrued.

I was in no hurry to find myself another job, despite Sally constantly nagging me to get off my backside. Now that she was the only breadwinner in our house, I reasoned that I could take on the role of housekeeper, looking after the place and fixing our meals. Sally showed some willingness to give my suggestion a try, but I never took to the role very well, and she soon became increasingly fed up by my lack of effort.

She gave me money for buying our food, but I used to spend at least half of this on booze. Being the saint that she was, she usually overlooked this, even funding some of my nightlife adventures with an occasional loan or two.

But as the months went on, and it became obvious to her that I wasn't showing any interest in getting back into work, our relationship became more and more uneasy.

I had been to the odd interview, and had taken part in a "back to work" training course, sponsored by the government. I'd had to, to keep my benefits coming. But no job had yet turned up that took my fancy—one that would pay what I thought I deserved, and support the sort of charmed lifestyle that I had had at the agency. I might have considered a job that involved travelling, or one that came with a car. Everything seemed much tougher now, but I wasn't going to allow myself to be sucked into any old job, just to get some wages.

Since getting a promotion, Sally was spending more time in the office. This was good news for me, as she was bringing more money in. But we saw much less of each other, and the nights when Sally used to join me to let loose on the town were long gone.

I told Sally about my various half-hearted attempts to find work, of course. I wanted her to believe that I was trying to get myself sorted, and that it wouldn't be long before I'd be able to start paying back her loans. It's clear to me now that she'd lost trust in me, and, perhaps because our sex was no longer as exciting as it once had been, she was quickly losing patience with me too.

Everything came to a head one Wednesday night, when she'd got home late after an exasperating meeting. I was slumped on the sofa as usual, feet sprawled over the pouffe in front of me, beer cans and my roll-ups stacked up on the side table to my right, and the remote controls for the TV and video lined up to my left. I heard the door slam as Sally entered the flat, and in the corner of my eye could see her pounding swiftly toward the bedroom behind me.

"What the fuck is this!" she screamed, storming into the sitting room, and hurling the new pair of jeans that I'd bought for myself earlier straight at my face. Admittedly, I'd gone a bit overboard with my purchase, going for the best Levi's that money can buy, but who shouldn't be able to treat themselves to the best once in a while?

"How much did these fucking things cost?" Sally demanded, quickly grabbing the still unsewn garment back and boxing me around the head with it.

"Not only do you sit around on your fat arse all day doing nothing, but you have the gall to go spending my money on stupid clothes that you've already got!"

Sally and I had rowed many times before, and especially recently, but this was the angriest that I'd seen her. I started to fumble a pathetic reply, but Sally was already grabbing at my T-shirt and pulling my hair.

"Get up, you lazy bastard!" she shrieked, "I've had enough! I'm not putting up with this madness any longer! I want you out of my house!"

I'd heard her make threats like this before, but never thought that she was serious. I stood up, and raised my hands defensively. "All right, all right, give me a break," I pleaded, "I just wanted to treat myself for once, that's all."

I thought Sally would back off, but she was close to boiling point. "You're always fucking treating yourself, always going to get to the next job that comes along, always going to start making more of an effort to clear up this place," she continued. "This time I've really had it! I mean it, Jack—you and me are finished!"

She went back into the bedroom. I sat back on the sofa, not really thinking that this was any more than one of our normal tiffs. "She'll calm down in a minute," I contented myself. "She's probably had a bad day at work."

Ten minutes later, Sally came back into the sitting room, trailing two loaded suitcases behind her. She opened the door that she'd slammed behind her just a little earlier, and proceeded to dump the bulging bags on the public landing outside.

"You've got five minutes to get out of this place," she said, now more calmly than before, but in a tone that made clear that she was serious. "There's your stuff," she said, pointing to the laden cases in the hall-way, "And this is where our relationship ends. We're finished!"

I felt as though I'd just been woken from an angry dream, but realised that Sally wasn't backing down. I made a vain attempt to plead for forgiveness, promising to make a fresh start, but she wouldn't even listen to me.

It was clear to me that I couldn't stay in the flat that night, so I collected the cases and set off for the streets of the West End, the throbbing thoroughfares that were so familiar to me. "Perhaps she'll see differently tomorrow," I mused, but this wasn't to be. Sally had quickly arranged for the door locks at the flat to be changed, and made herself uncontactable to me at work.

For the first time in my life, I found myself homeless, and with barely enough coppers to pay for a coffee. It was at least mid-summer, and the nights were warm. I'd managed to salvage a few off-cuts of unwanted chipboard from a builder's skip, and set myself up a crude shelter in Lincolns Inn Fields, which had become something of a shanty town for the homeless in the mid 80's.

This was a good spot for mixing with others who could teach me a few things about living rough, and the square was visited nightly by the Salvation Army's mobile soup kitchen.

I survived on the streets for six months, before the cold of winter began to take its toll. I contracted what I later learned was a severe form of pneumonia, and had been rushed into Bart's Hospital when one of the Sally's Army volunteers saw me shivering and wheezing. I spent several weeks in intensive care in Bart's, and then was offered a temporary stay in a refuge for the homeless.

I suppose this period of enforced rest was meant to be. It certainly proved to be something of a turning point for me.

I realised that the life of Reilly that I'd been living when I was at the agency wasn't an experience that most people enjoyed. I'd been carried by Sally for too long, having no sense of responsibility for myself or for money. All I'd wanted to do was enjoy myself, never thinking about the consequences. How could I have been so naive? Somewhat late in the day, I suppose, I was finally coming to see what an idiot I'd been.

The people at the refuge were kind to me, and didn't judge me for the life that I'd led. One of them in particular, a counsellor called Maggie, spent hours with me, trying to help me build up my confidence again and find a way forward.

I was pretty sure that I was going to take a different tack if I had another chance. Maggie worked alongside others who helped people who were down on their luck get back on their feet, and she found out about a job that she thought might interest me, working for a bookmaker.

The charity helped me smarten myself up, even giving me a loan so that I could buy myself a suit. This was one loan that I didn't squander on booze. I was determined to give my best at the interview—for Maggie and her friends, if not for myself.

I liked the idea of being a bookie, and obviously said enough at the interview, because I was offered the job there and then. I was put through a period of training, and then started what was a sort of apprenticeship, working to my manager, Mr. Lyons.

Mr. Lyons was a good boss, but he took no nonsense. I didn't mess around like I had before, taking days off as sick leave when I felt like it, or drifting in late. I revelled in what I was learning, and enjoyed dealing with the punters.

The later shifts that I started to work gave me quite a bit of freedom, allowing me to frequent some of my old night-time haunts again, while having time the next morning to nurse my hangover before heading back into the shop.

Mr. Lyons seemed pleased with my progress, and after six months, he considered me safe enough to occasionally leave in the shop alone. It felt good to be trusted again, and I was sure that I'd really turned a corner since the time I'd been squatting in the Fields.

I got to know many of the regular punters who came into the shop. Most of them just enjoyed having a little flutter, a way of creating a bit of excitement for themselves. Sometimes they got lucky, sometimes not. Always they had a story to tell about how their accumulator nearly made them a small fortune, or offered a tip for a race later in the day.

When the races were showing on the TV screens around the shop, there'd usually be a few of the regulars cheering their horses or dogs on. I suppose it was no different really to being at the actual race itself.

I was happiest when paying out the winnings for punters who'd got lucky. While I sympathized when their bets went wrong, as they usually did, I'd been told by Mr. Lyons to not get involved with any of them on a personal level. "Be sensitive, but no more," he'd warned me.

My job was simple enough, taking bets and handling payments. Everything was strictly done to order, as Mr. Lyons had shown me. The adrenaline that everyone felt when a big race began was unlike anything I can describe. You couldn't help feel the excitement of the punters who'd gambled beyond their normal wagers. If gambling is a bug, then I was seriously in danger of catching it.

I started playing along with the betting, although not actually risking money myself, which wasn't allowed by the company. I used to pick a horse or a dog before a race, willing them on and feeling very excited when they crossed the finish line first. But it wasn't long before I thought that it was time for this "sport", as I liked to call my simple indulgence, to move up a level.

I didn't plan to be reckless with my flutters, just to play with a little amount that I'd set aside. At first, I used to stop by a rival bookie to place my bets, sometimes acting on tips that punters had mentioned to me in the shop. My little venture more or less broke even, and I even had one or two quite profitable wins.

I knew that I mustn't go back to my old days of spending mindlessly, but my early success as a gambler boosted my confidence, and I started exploring what the West End's casinos had to offer. I didn't care for the big table games like roulette and blackjack. But for only a small handful of change, I could keep myself happy playing the one arm bandit machines.

To get the best out of these involved having a degree of knowledge about how the machines actually worked, as well as a level of skill to know when to nudge or hold a reel before it landed on a spot that was guaranteed to pay out money. We had several of these machines in the shop, and I'd often cast an eye over punters when they were playing them.

At the casino, I always set myself up in front of the same machine, playing with the smallest coins that it would accept as I studied its patterns of behaviour. I might as well have been in a relationship with a woman. In a way, I suppose, I was.

My machine–"Betty", as I called her–started to do me proud. I'd kept a close record of how much I'd spent, and how much she paid out, noting the patterns that I knew I could nudge to steal a prize. Soon, Betty was beginning to pay me back everything that I fed into her.

I started to visit the casino most nights, feeding larger offerings into Betty's narrow, stainless steel mouth. I was aware that I was being watched, but the casino management wouldn't be concerned with small fry such as myself. They'd know what sums I was playing with when they came to empty the machine, even though I was slowly giving more and more of my earnings up to Betty's belly.

I was certain that, sooner or later, I would be able to do more than break even on my little project, and that before long, I'd be firmly in the driving seat.

To say that I was breaking even isn't strictly correct. I wasn't losing large sums, for sure, but I usually ended up being slightly out of pocket after each visit to the casino.

The problem for me was the one that's familiar to all gamblers–knowing when to stop. If I'd had a good win, was slightly up on what I'd fed into Betty and hoped that my winning streak would continue, I'd give her more. If I struck lucky, I'd not want to give up on my winning streak; if I drew a blank, I reasoned that my next pull of Betty's arm would come up trumps. I never learned that there's a right moment to walk away.

Mr. Lyons wasn't aware of my visits to the casino, but he started to notice that something was bothering me. I was so engrossed in my affair with Betty, that I'd barely noticed that I was losing touch with my home life.

I'd managed quite well to care for myself in the small bedsit that I'd rented since settling into the job.

I'd bought several things on a "buy now, pay later" basis, still others using my credit cards. I felt that I needed to treat myself for getting back on my feet—a new TV and video, a top-of-the-range hi-fi, and various other "essentials" that would make my tiny squat a place worth spending time in.

Even though I didn't yet admit it to myself, I must have known deep down that, sooner or later, these bills were going to have to be paid. I'd managed to keep some repayments going by taking out new loans, but was no longer being offered credit by the banks. It seemed that my only option for keeping afloat was to take out a loan with a backstreet merchant, of which there were many around Soho. I didn't stop to think about what I was doing.

Within weeks of taking out a loan with one of these shady dealers, I received a letter demanding an immediate interest repayment for almost half of what I'd taken out. I couldn't believe what I was reading. I hid the letter among my files, hoping that I wouldn't be bothered again for another few weeks, by which time I might have been able to work out a way of paying back the money.

A month later, I received another letter, noting my first non-payment and adding a further hundred percent to the first month's interest, not to mention another outrageous amount for the month that had just passed. A letter threatening action being taken against me followed a short while later, after I again failed to make a payment by the required time.

I was now panicking, and my anxiety started to show at work. Mr. Lyons picked me up several times for mistakes that I'd made with the books, but he seemed to want to know if anything was troubling me. I thanked him for his concern, but decided against letting on about what was preoccupying my mind.

One of my duties at the shop was to empty the machines each night. The money was bagged up and kept in the safe at the back of the store. The takings were recorded, but weren't reconciled with the cash that our security people transported from the safe to the bank until the end of each month.

It occurred to me that, if my timing was right, I had a chance to get myself out of the trouble that I was in. My thinking was that if I borrowed some of the cash that I took out of the machines to pay off my loan, then I could get another loan to pay back the money that I'd taken before the money in the safe was taken to the bank.

My plan seemed the only option for avoiding another letter from the loan company, and so I set about putting it into action. I paid off my loan, and then took out a further loan with another backstreet provider to top up the money that was kept in the safe.

All appeared to have gone well until a few days later, when I was called aside by Mr. Lyons.

He came straight out with what he wanted to know. "What on earth have you been doing, taking cash from the machine?" he demanded.

I was astonished that I'd been found out. I couldn't work out who could have seen me switch the money, given that I'd been the only person in the shop at the time. Still, I decided to come clean about my clandestine activities.

"I'm so sorry, Mr. Lyons. I hold my hands up to this. I needed to borrow some cash urgently to pay off a loan, but I've already paid it back."

"I'm sorry lad, but we're going to have to let you go. You know the rules–no taking or borrowing money from the machine. The matter is out of my hands. The whole thing was recorded on video, and head office didn't hang around in making their decision. I'm sorry."

I could see that Mr. Lyons would have been ready to give me another chance if he'd been able to, but in my desperate state of mind, I'd broken one company policy that must never be broken. I did know the rules, and I'd fallen foul of them.

Mr. Lyons wished me well, and thanked me for the good work that I had done. He even gave me a firm hug as we said our goodbyes, the kind that a father might give to his son. I felt myself welling up with painful emotion in that moment, but I didn't let myself cry.

I was devastated to have to leave the shop, and walked out onto the street in a state of shock. Barely able to make sense of where I was, I headed to the reliable welcome of the only friend I knew, Betty.

Not only had I just lost my job, my only source of income for paying my rent, but I still had debts to pay, including the new loan that I'd taken out to fund my raid on the shop's machine. As before, if I couldn't find a way of paying this back soon, I'd quickly be facing threatening letters again.

"Betty, what am I going to do?" I asked, as I pulled on her sturdy arm.

Betty answered by paying out a small collection of silver.

"Of course! Why didn't I see it before! Betty, you are my salvation!"

In my confused and troubled state, I convinced myself that I now had the knowledge and skill to make Betty work for me. I dropped another coin into her slot, and–bingo!–she paid out again. It seemed as though Betty really understood my predicament, almost as though she was playing her part to help me.

With newfound confidence, I decided to really put Betty to the test. I spent a frantic hour pouring all the money that I had into Betty's slot, sure that I was only moments away from finally freeing her of her big prize.

I saw the reels turn to patterns that I recognised, knowing that I was just a few nudges away from what I was sure would bring Betty to her climax. "Just one more nudge...just one more...and then I've made it!" But my money ran out too soon, and Betty held on to the last piece of silver that I fed into her.

My loan provider wasted no time in seeking amends for the payments that I'd let pass. Early one Friday morning some three months later, two brawny gentlemen arrived at my door, advising me that they had a right to take possessions from me in lieu of payments that I'd failed to make. In the space of thirty minutes, all of my earthly possessions were taken from me.

One month later, my landlord served an order for possession of the bedsit that had been my home, which I'd not been able to pay rent for over several months. I was given two weeks in which to leave the property.

And so I again found myself homeless and almost penniless.

How could I have been so foolish to allow myself to take out such ridiculous loans, just to fill my house with fancy gadgets? I'd started off so well in controlling my spending since leaving the refuge, but how quickly my greed had got the better of me.

I had tired of London, and decided to take a cheap bus to Brighton, hoping that a different chapter might open up for me there. I joined the homeless who set up their pitches in the porches of the large stores along North Street, the main street that runs through the centre. During the daytime, I ambled around, occasionally resting on one of the canopied benches that line the promenade. Being near the sea was good for me–all of that space and fresh air.

Begging usually earned me enough coppers each day to buy myself something to eat, usually a sandwich or some other perishable that a supermarket was selling off cheap before closing. Warm food was the best if I could get it, especially as winter approached.

I soon got to know some of the volunteers who handed out the mugs of soup each night. One of them told me that I could apply for a place in a night shelter that was being offered by several churches over the Christmas period. The bout of pneumonia that I'd come down with before marked me out as someone who was thought to be vulnerable in the cold, and so I was offered a place in the shelter.

I enjoyed the company of my fellow wanderers during my stay in the shelter. Our camp beds were moved each night from church hall to church hall, meaning that we had to make our way across town during the day. A wholesome supper was laid on every night, and we were given breakfast before setting out onto the streets again each morning.

There were rules, of course–no drugs, no needles, and no fighting. But I was determined not to get involved in any monkey business this time, keeping my head down as much as I could.

All I wanted was another chance to make something of myself. I'd spent too many nights sleeping rough.

Michael, one of the helpers that I met during my time in the shelter, suggested that I tried to apply for a place in a hostel that he worked with. Places there were limited, but I might be in with a chance of being taken on, given my risk of going down with pneumonia again if I ventured back onto the streets.

Michael's suggestion gave me fresh hope. If I could get a bed in the hostel, I would have an address that I could use when I began looking for work. If I could get work, after a time, I might be able to look for my own place–possibly a small flat let out by the council. Once I had my own home and a job, anything would be possible.

Michael helped me fill out my application, and introduced me to the hostel warden. The warden said that there would be no problem with me being registered with the hostel, but there were no spare beds free for newcomers. My name was added to a long waiting list, and I found myself back on the streets at a freezing start to the new year.

Apart from begging, I didn't know what I could do to earn myself a small amount of cash. Being homeless, I couldn't claim benefits, and no one was going to give me a job. It was the same problem for everyone who lived rough.

At times, I felt that I wanted to walk out into the dark waters that pounded the beach, letting the waves cover me. It would only take a matter of minutes for me to die from hypothermia, if I didn't drown first, and then it would all be over.

But I was determined not to give up hope. The small change that I earned from begging meant that I didn't starve. Still, I longed for the days when I was able to collect a pay packet every month.

I started thinking about what work I might be able to do if I was given a chance by the hostel. I always fancied being a long distance lorry driver, and started to research how I might train for a heavy goods licence once I'd saved a little money from the benefits that I'd then be able to claim.

The early months of the new year proved to be much colder than December had been. Overnight temperatures often fell below freezing, driving me almost to a point that I couldn't bear. The porches of the stores where I rested at night offered me some shelter from the wind, but gave no respite from the snow and ice that now covered the streets.

I felt my coughing and vomiting coming again. One night, my heartbeat rose to a point where I thought my heart was about to explode. My shivering worsened. I don't know exactly how it happened, but I fell unconscious for a long time, almost as though I was in a coma.

I was found the next morning by workers when they arrived to open up the shop that I was lying in front of. When they were unable to wake me to ask me to move on, they realized that something was wrong and so they called for an ambulance.

I spent a week in the Royal Sussex County Hospital, receiving treatment for pneumonia and hypothermia. Michael visited me regularly, and promised to speak again with the hostel, to see if anything could be done to speed up my application for a bed there.

"Pray for me," I pleaded with him, finding myself asking for something that I'd never done before. "Don't you worry, Jack." he promised, "I will."

I also tried to cry out for help. "God, angels, whoever you are. If you can hear me, please, I need your help. Please get me out of this life I've got myself into. I know that I only have myself to blame. I promise not to let you down if you will help me."

Michael arrived later the next morning. He had had a long discussion with the warden at the hostel, and they'd managed to find me a bed, justifying moving me off the waiting list because of my current situation. The hospital had wanted to discharge me as quickly as possible, but was anxious to know if my carers could do anything to avoid me being put back onto the streets.

I couldn't believe my good fortune. "Michael," I mumbled quietly, "Can I tell you a secret?"

"Of course you can, Jack. That's what I'm here for."

"Do you remember when I asked you to pray for me last night?" I continued. Michael nodded.

"Well, I also prayed for a miracle to happen. And if this isn't a miracle, I don't know what is!" Michael smiled, and cupped his hands around mine.

"Sometimes we just have to wait for a new door to open," he said with a benevolent eye. "But I think that God knows that you've waited long enough."

⇢⇦

I stuck to my plan after moving into the hostel, saving every penny from my benefits cheque to pay for my driver training. Within three months, I'd signed up for the course, and after another three months had earned my heavy goods licence. It didn't take me long to be hired by a haulage company, and a short while later, I was offered a chance to move into a small council-let flat.

That was all two years ago now. I've kept on the straight and narrow. My days of reckless spending are long behind me, and I've kept saving as much as I can. I've clocked up nearly 150,000 miles in the cab now. I know where I'm going–keeping my eyes firmly fixed ahead of me, sticking to the road that I know I must follow.

Afterword

The story of *The three little pigs* teaches that those who spend all of their time pursuing pleasure, without making provision for a future when they might face difficulty, usually seal their own fate. A life of 'sex, drugs, and rock and roll' guarantees pleasure only for the short term.

Thinking, planning, and resourcefulness are usually required to assure a comfortable future. In our modern world, this is perhaps most obviously demonstrated by the large number of people who find themselves struggling to pay off loans that they've accumulated with credit cards.

There is evidence of progression in facing up to the challenge of laying down a solid foundation for life seen in the response taken by the middle pig compared with that of his elder sibling. But his stick-built house is also hastily thrown together, leaving maximum time free for eating and indulging his greed.

The youngest pig is thoughtful and hard working, and, of course, thinks carefully about how he can outwit the wolf. Not only does this pig's house stand-up against the wolf's desperate attempts to destroy it, but the pig survives another four plots that are hatched by the wolf to entrap him.

However, the young pig doesn't deny himself all pleasure, taking up each of the wolf's suggestions for gathering food. He doesn't idly waste time picking all of the turnips, nor hang around for longer than he needs to in the branches of the apple tree or during his visit to the market. He knows when to allow himself to seek out these pleasures, setting out early to find them, but not impulsively grabbing at them as soon as the wolf mentions them.

Instead, the pig continues to think through his situation, doing his best to understand what might be going on in the mind of the wolf. While the wolf is physically capable of devouring the pig in an instant, his good sense allows him to ultimately defeat this powerful foe.

The choice of construction for the three houses is sometimes pointed to as being symbolic of human-kind's progress. In earlier times, we built houses of mud and straw, later discovering that wooden shelters were often more sturdy. Only in more recent times, when bricks have been mass-produced, have most houses being made from strong masonry.

It's possible to see that the development of person-ality, as presented through the experiences of the three pigs, might be observed in a single person. Indeed, this is possibly what the author of the original story in-tended.

If we are able to shed those aspects of our person-ality that lead us into trouble, can learn from our ex-periences, and take fresh decisions that make use of our learnings, then we might be able to grow and con-quer any adversary or obstacle that might stand in our way.

The development of the three pigs' personalities is a topic of interest for several commentators. Those who've probed for psychological meaning in the story suggest that we might see a development from a personality that's influenced by the *id*, through to one in which the *superego* has a bearing[6].

The older pigs project their carnal natures onto the wolf, especially their preference to devour. With the younger pig, there's a stark contrast with the wolf–one displaying virtuous attributes, the other ignoble. It is the older pigs' devouring natures, if it is unconscious to them, which leads to them being consumed.

---

[6] The *id* and *superego* are two of three aspects of a person's psyche that were envisaged by Sigmund Freud. The *id* is the most primitive component, responding on instinct and seeking immediate satisfaction; the *superego* puts control on the *id*–for example, ensuring that a person isn't driven by pure sexual impulse. The third component of the psyche described by Freud, the *ego*, influences decisions on how an individual behaves, taking account of what is realistic and socially acceptable. In the story of *The three little pigs*, the *ego* still holds sway for the youngest pig, while he has developed a stronger moral compass than his brothers (an aspect of the *superego*).

Goldilocks and the three bears

Long ago, in a distant land, there once lived a girl named Goldilocks. She had been given her name because her hair was pure gold in colour, and her curly locks reached right down to her shoulders.

Goldilocks didn't enjoy spending all her days at home, preferring to be outside exploring things.

One day, while she was chasing butterflies and admiring many beautiful flowers, Goldilocks started to wander out into the middle of a wood. This was a place that she'd never visited before.

After a while, she came to a clearing in the trees, where there stood a charming little cottage. Smoke was billowing from its chimney, and Goldilocks noticed that the door to the house was open. She thought that she might wander over, to see if she might discover what sort of person might live in such a house.

The cottage belonged to three bears–father, mother and their little son. The family had left their porridge to cool in the kitchen, while they took their morning walk through the woods.

Goldilocks peered around the door of the cottage, but couldn't see that anyone was at home. The tiny house was silent, but for the crackle of the fire, which sputtered heartily in the kitchen.

Goldilocks fancied that she might enter the house, to see what she might discover.

She came into the kitchen, where she noticed three bowls of porridge on the table, waiting to be eaten. Feeling hungry, Goldilocks decided that she would like to taste a little of the porridge for herself.

She first tried eating from the largest of the three bowls, which belonged to Father Bear.

"Oh, this is far too cold!" cried Goldilocks, after taking a mouth full from the bowl. "Let me try another bowl!"

She then proceeded to scoop a spoonful of porridge from the medium sized bowl, which belonged to Mother Bear.

"Oh, this is much too hot!" Goldilocks screamed, before noticing the smallest of the bowls on the table– the one that belonged to Little Bear.

Once more, Goldilocks took a mouthful of porridge, and this time, was well satisfied.

"This porridge is just right!" she said to herself, and then proceeded to gobble up all of Little Bear's porridge.

After she had eaten, Goldilocks thought that she would like to explore the cottage further. She came into the parlour room, where she noticed three chairs, each of a different size.

She first tried sitting in the largest of the three chairs, which belonged to Father Bear.

"Oh, this chair is too high!" Goldilocks called out, hopping off the chair to try the next largest of the three, which belonged to Mother Bear.

"Oh, this chair is too broad!" cried Goldilocks, and she again hopped out of the chair.

Finally, Goldilocks tried sitting in the smallest of the three chairs, which belonged to Little Bear.

"Oh, this is just right!" said Goldilocks. But she was too heavy for the chair, and it quickly broke into many pieces.

Feeling very tired, Goldilocks decided that she would venture upstairs, hoping to find a bedchamber where she might be able to have a little rest.

Finding the bear's chamber, she saw that she had three beds to choose from—each of different sizes.

First of all, Goldilocks jumped onto the biggest of the three beds, which belonged to Father Bear.

"Oh, this is too hard!" screamed Goldilocks, jumping off the bed and on to the medium-sized bed that lay next to it, which belonged to Mother Bear.

"Oh, this is too soft!" cried Goldilocks, and she again hopped off the bed.

Finally, Goldilocks lay down on the smallest of the three beds, which belonged to Little Bear.

"Oh, this is just right!" Goldilocks uttered to herself, and, feeling contented, she very soon fell into a lovely sleep.

While she was sleeping, the three bears finished their walk, and made their way home to eat their porridge.

When they arrived in the kitchen, they were surprised to see that someone had paid them a visit.

Seeing that a spoonful of porridge had been scooped from his bowl, Father Bear uttered, "Someone's been tasting my porridge!"

Mother Bear noticed the same, announcing, "Someone's been tasting my porridge!"

Finally, Little Bear looked at his bowl, and then bewailed, "Someone's been tasting my porridge, and they've eaten it all up!"

The bears then went into the parlour. Noticing that the cushion on his chair had been moved, Father Bear growled, "Someone's been sitting in my chair!"

Mother Bear noticed the same, and pronounced, "Someone's been sitting in my chair!"

Finally, Little Bear took a look at his chair and cried, "Someone's been sitting in my chair, and has broken it all up!"

The bears then decided to go upstairs, to see if they might learn more about the mystery of who had been eating their porridge and sitting in their chairs.

Entering the bedchamber, Father Bear immediately noticed that the cover of his bed had been ruffled. "Someone's been lying on my bed!" he observed.

Mother Bear noticed that her pillow had been moved, declaring, "Someone's been lying on my bed!"

Finally, Little Bear went over to his bed and screamed, "Someone's been lying on my bed, and here she is!"

Hearing Little Bear's screaming, Goldilocks woke up from her sleep. Seeing the three Bears staring at her, Goldilocks was very frightened. She quickly made for the window, from which she jumped onto the ground below.

Goldilocks ran as fast as she could back through the wood.

Never again did she venture near the bear's comfortable little home.

THE FOURTH TALE–CHAPTER TWO

Tough love

No parent would ever want to have a child like me. Throughout my life, I've battled to be accepted. Holding on to my self-respect has been difficult, and at times, my faith in myself has withered to having virtually none at all.

Others call me a "mutant", or a "freak", or just a plain "weirdo". It's always been this way, ever since I started school. While the other kids were learning how to read and write, my only interest was being left alone to draw. I loved drawing action heroes, supermen and martial arts masters. When I drew, I could escape the pulling of my red hair and the taunting that the other kids doled out on me.

It's not easy being a weirdo, but when you learn that this is the way the world sees you, you try to make the best of it. My trouble was that I couldn't read and write. My teacher told me that I needed help to be able to even pronounce some words. So I was sent to a special school, where they taught lessons in elocution and helped us slower kids learn how to spell our names and, eventually, to read and write.

Most of my time at school bored me, but I loved pouring over the pictures in the books in the school library. The colours excited me, and the inky pages smelt wonderful.

I still saw some of the kids from my first school. We used to belong to the same scout group, which my parents had insisted I joined to help me mix in with others of my own age. They didn't know what went on during those Tuesday evenings in the church hall.

I was always the butt of everyone's jokes, and often the subject of a devilish prank, that brought great pleasure to the others. I suppose that since I was marked out as the *persona non grata* in the group, no one else need fear that they might be considered an outsider. Benny-bashing was their way of proving themselves to be members of the gang, united by a common cause—to make my life hell.

There was no end to the vicious games that they devised. I had my eyebrows singed, and my pubic hair shaved off. A drawing that I had worked on for a competition organised by the Roundtable was covered in red paint when it was put on display for judging.

I was always called last when teams were selected for games in the park, and no one ever called me by my first name. I was always "Bendy Benny", or "Benny, whose missing a penny," or most commonly of all, simply a "fucking wanker".

My parents knew some of what was going on, but they thought it best that I learned to stand up for myself. "Boys will be boys," was all that they'd been told when they reported their concerns to the scout troop leader. This was of course true. What they didn't appreciate–and what I didn't then realise myself–was that I was far from capable of standing on my own two feet.

I enjoyed my new school. The teachers were kind to me, and most of the other kids there were oddballs like me. Only once did I nearly get into trouble, when I'd decided to wander into the headmaster's office. It was break-time, and I knew that the headmaster had taken his mug of coffee to watch over what was happening in the playground.

I wondered what it would be like to be in charge of the school, and so pushed open his office door, plonking myself on the big wooden chair behind his desk. I sat up straight and imagined myself giving orders to all of the school. But in truth, I didn't feel too comfortable in this position, and found the chair too high for my liking too.

While I was dreaming about being in charge of all that went on at *St. Bernadette of Lourdes*, the study door was suddenly pushed open. In came the headmaster, returning unexpectedly early from his tour of the playground.

I slipped out from his seat and crept under his desk, I think just before he noticed that there was a stranger in his office. To my relief, he simply placed his empty coffee mug back on his desk, before retracing his steps back to the playground. I quickly followed close behind him.

When I reached fourteen, I had to leave the special needs school, since the classes there were really meant for younger children. I didn't want to leave–I enjoyed playing with the model cars and joining in with the younger kids, but I knew that at some point I had to face up to moving on from my childhood.

"You'll do very well at big school," my teacher told me. I'd grown very fond of her, and trusted her more than anyone. "Keep up with your reading, and never give any attention to what the other boys and girls say to you."

When I left the school that had taught me how to read and to write, my teacher gave me a set of special ink drawing pens, as an encouragement to continue with my art. That was one of the happiest days of my life, of which there have been very few.

My new school was worse than I'd feared. I tried to take my former teacher's advice, ignoring the taunts that kept coming from before the first bell of the morning until I was walking home at night. It didn't help that I'd joined the school three full years later than most of the other kids, all of whom seemed to be happily settled into their tightly formed friendships and little gangs.

I was quickly told that I walked strangely, while my stutter was a cause for constant amusement in the playground. I tried to ignore the attention that I was given, walking in silence around the playground during break times, or burying my head in a book in the library.

There were times when I was set upon, but the constant threat of punishment dissuaded some from taking advantage of me. On more than one occasion, I found myself being picked up off the ground by a group of older boys, being turned upside down and then lowered into a filthy waste-bin, my head becoming like a sticking-plaster for used ice-lolly wrappers and the debris of a dozen crisp packets. "You're rubbish, Selby!" I'd be told. "Rubbish! Rubbish! Rubbish!"

After such incidents, I would have no easy explanation for my mother when she demanded to know why my blazer was covered in muck. She'd shout at me, and call me stupid for not even knowing how I'd managed to get my uniform into such a state, but I think she really knew that I felt too embarrassed to tell her that I'd been picked upon again.

I struggled with most of my coursework, and was lampooned in class by most of my teachers. It wasn't that I couldn't remember what was being said, but simply that I couldn't see the point of what I was learning. My attention quickly used to wander during lessons. I longed to be back in the art room, working on my drawings.

The one subject other than art that I excelled at was mathematics. I loved the challenge of working out the tough problems that Mr Bloch, my maths teacher, would set, and I came to see that the formula that were scratched on the blackboard had a kind of beauty that was all their own. I was always given top grades for maths, and found a friend in Mr Bloch, who would often intervene when it was his turn to patrol the playground, whenever I was being bundled to the ground by a riotous mob, or became the target for a fast-moving football in a painful close-contact game of "Kick Selby".

At our school, everyone except me seemed to know everything about sex. Some of my classmates were already dating, and everything from condoms to dildos had been confiscated for the headmistress's safekeeping. I liked to brag about girls that I would like to shag, hoping that this might allow me to join in the banter that preoccupied the other boys' time, possibly even letting me become accepted by them. It didn't, and if I'm honest, everything that I said was made up.

I had started to wet the bed even before I started at the big school, and I became easily excited whenever I overheard anyone talking about sex.

While I tried to imagine what it might be like to be with a girl, I had no real idea what went on behind closed doors. I was fascinated by the blossoming bodies of some of the girls in my class, and thought that I might fancy one or two of them, but my thoughts about being in love didn't go beyond a naive fantasy of romance.

I didn't even know if I would enjoy physical contact. I didn't like being touched by my parents, so why should I feel any differently about being in close contact with anyone else?

Since I had no prospect of finding a girl at school who would go out with me, I satisfied myself that my time would come later. But still it seemed that I would be the last in my year to lose my virginity, and that thought troubled me a lot.

Had I not been so concerned about creating an impression of interest in "normal sex", I might have done better at that time to explore my sexuality. After all, if I'd turned out to be a homo or a pervert, I had little to lose in terms of my social standing, given that I was the pariah of the whole school.

I even wondered if things might have been easier had I been born a girl. I thought that perhaps girls were less prone to being bullied in the way that I was, and that their peers may more easily tolerate any awkwardness that they might show. That, at least, was my naive way of thinking at that time. I need only have looked at the experiences of one or two of the less popular girls in my class to realise that my perception was far from the truth.

On one occasion, I was set upon by a group of girls and taken to the girls' toilet block. There, I was stripped to my underwear and made to wear a dress that one of my kidnappers had smuggled into the school. One of the girls even smeared lipstick on my face, and attempted a rush job at brushing my eyelashes with her mascara wand. It was horrible.

The gang then used some old pantyhose to tie my hands to the piping that ran around a part of the top of the cubicle in which their hilarious prank was enacted. "He's loving it," they shouted, as they backed away sniggering. "Selby the wanker is loving it!"

Once I'd managed to free myself from the light ties of the pantyhose and escaped the cubicle, I stood staring at myself in the washroom mirror. "What a total mess," I thought to myself, as I hurriedly tried to wash the lipstick off. I didn't look right in a dress. But I didn't feel totally ill at ease either.

My schooling ended when I reached eighteen. While I had flunked most of my exams at sixteen, I'd been allowed to continue with my studies as I'd excelled in my maths exam. The same opportunity came to me when I was offered a place to read mathematics at Edinburgh University. I started the following October, when my parents drove me the three hundred miles to settle into my new accommodation.

My old teacher at *St. Bernadette of Lourdes* was thrilled when I wrote to inform her that I'd been offered a place at Edinburgh. No one from the school had ever been accepted by a university before.

I had been looking forward to starting my degree. For the first time in my life, I had a room of my own, in a hall of residence that was close to the main campus. My parents were three hundred miles away, and nobody in this city knew me. I felt that now was my big chance for making a fresh start. I thought that I could perhaps put what I'd learnt during my formative years to my advantage.

I settled in well during my first few weeks in the hall. I introduced myself to others who, like me, had arrived not knowing anyone. At first, most seemed happy to join me for meals in the hall's refectory. At last, I thought, I had the chance to make friends. For once too, no one was taunting me, nor trying to crush my self-dignity.

I took my studies seriously, and soon was earning good marks for my assignments. I never missed a class, and worked hard to please my tutor.

One or two of the people that I met at the hall started to ask me to share coffee with them in their rooms. I also started to join one or two of the clubs that were organised by the student union. As a student, it didn't feel too bad to be a weirdo, because most of my fellow undergraduates seemed to be no less weird than me.

While I wasn't humiliated, after a while I realised that only a few people seemed to really want to get to know me. I once overheard one of them talking to another classmate who was organising a party.

"Please ask Benny to your party," my friend asked. "He's a real oddball, but it would mean so much to him. Everyone else is coming."

I did get invited to the party, but what I'd overheard gave me the first clue that even those who I considered to be close friends thought me to be a little strange.

I had no idea how to behave at a party, having never been invited to one before. I felt unsure how to break the ice with people that I'd never met, and so decided to take some liquid courage, and proceeded to fill cup after cup for myself from the punch bowl.

I've no idea what they put in that stuff, but before most of the guests had even arrived, I was struggling to keep my focus–finding myself laughing and shouting, blundering from one interrupted conversation to another.

The crowded space of people talking in front of me soon started to clear, but I contented myself by continuing to steady my nerves with the punch, while helping myself to the assorted dips and savoury foods that were laid out nearby. Unaware that I could no longer keep my balance, I fell back against the trestle table that served as a bar for the drinks, causing the whole ensemble to collapse.

I'm not sure what I might have said when I was helped to my feet, and even less what might have been said to me. What I do know is that my next memory was after waking up the following morning, noticing that I'd vomited all over the carpet, and feeling that my head was about to explode.

I wrote a letter to the party host to apologise for my actions, and reasoned to myself that my behaviour wasn't out of keeping for a young, fun-seeking student such as myself. But no more party invitations followed after that night, and I began to sense that most of my peers were giving me a wide berth whenever they saw me approaching. Even the few people that I still regarded as friends started to distance themselves from me, making excuses whenever I suggested getting together.

One person who didn't ignore me completely was Ellie. I'd met Ellie and her large group of friends at the student union's jazz club. She lived in the same hall as me, and we often met over breakfast.

At the time, I thought that Ellie had taken a liking to me. Looking back, I can see now that she'd noticed that I was a loner, and had taken sympathy on me by trying to involve me in her gang.

Ellie had many friends, who would gather in each other's rooms to share jokes or listen to music. She seemed to be very confident, and I enjoyed being around her. Her friends didn't seem to mind me joining their circle, although I probably over-estimated their welcome.

I didn't feel easy being in a large group, and didn't know how to start a conversation. Unlike others in the group, I didn't have a partner. I wasn't keen to accept the pipe that they used to pass around the room, with its strange mixture of what I thought was tobacco, although I soon grew to love its rich aroma.

What I wanted was to share time with Ellie alone, or with just one or two of her other friends. I thought that she might help me build my confidence, and perhaps allow me to feel more comfortable around women. Ellie's smiling and teasing seemed well intentioned, and I thought that we'd established a good rapport.

One small obstacle to developing a close friendship with Ellie was that she had a boyfriend, a mature student called Grant. She spent most of her free time with him, and wasn't shy about telling the group about the various new sex positions that they'd tried out together, nor sharing what ideas she meant to put into practice with him later that night.

I felt jealous, but was sure that Ellie's relationship shouldn't serve as an impediment to her building a good friendship with me.

In my room, I spent many hours thinking about Ellie, and wondering how I was going to find a girlfriend. I still didn't know what I would do if ever I found myself alone with a girl, nor whether I would actually enjoy doing any more than just kissing and cuddling.

I wasn't the only oddball on campus. University attracted all sorts of misfits and social pariahs. One other such loner was Pablo, a neighbour of mine in the hall. He was a member of the gay society, and one day he asked me if I would like to come to one of their meetings, to see if this may be something that I might enjoy.

I had my reservations about accepting his invitation, but since I received so few offers to join in anything, I agreed to go along.

The meeting itself was not very interesting. A group of about fifteen men and five women sat around in a circle, talking about their experiences, while progressively getting more and more drunk. I listened carefully as some of those present described the tender affection that they'd enjoyed with their partners. There seemed to be nothing disturbing about this, and I began to appreciate that one or two of the men who were sitting around the room were attractive to my eyes too.

Lars, a third-year classics student who was sitting next to me, put his arm around my shoulder as the discussion and consumption of wine progressed. I felt uneasy with this, but no less so than were it my arm that had wrapped its way around the shoulder of a woman.

As the meeting closed, Lars turned to me, and planted a small kiss on my cheek. "You're quite a cutie, young Benny," he whispered, in a deep, soft voice. I didn't know how to respond, but politely smiled and waited for my chance to bid him good night.

I didn't join Pablo at the club again, but I was troubled that I didn't feel able to relax with the likes of Lars, not being able to free myself sufficiently from my preconceptions about what I thought was "not normal sex" to properly explore whether this might be a lifestyle that could work for me.

My thoughts returned to Ellie. I decided that I had nothing to lose by asking her whether she would like to come out on a date with me, not taking a moment to consider that her relationship with Grant might make this difficult for her. I'm not sure what I hoped might result from a shared evening with Ellie. I just wanted to spend time with her, and felt that my knowledge and confidence with the opposite sex could only benefit by being around her.

Unsurprisingly, Ellie politely refused my invitation, gently explaining that she thought that Grant might feel uneasy about her spending time with another man.

Disappointed, I replied that I understood, though of course I did not.

Ellie had at least described me as a *man*. Perhaps this was a mistake, but it wasn't a label that had been given to me before. I had no real concept of what it meant to be a man. As far as I was concerned, I was just a young student, fresh out of high school, starting to learn the ways of the world. I was still coming to grips with the thrills and demands of adulthood, as it were.

I reflected on how I should behave were I to live up to the attribution that Ellie had honoured me with. I thought about my own father, who had been a boxer when he was in the army. He had a physical strength that I never thought I could equal, and was a very able mechanic and a gifted worker with wood. These were the sorts of skills and attributes that I thought were necessary to earn the right to be called a man. In my naive thinking, men enjoyed fighting, playing football, and making great displays of bravado. I could relate to none of this. Neither could I see myself as being a father to someone who depended upon me, nor a worthy husband for a wife.

As I reflected upon my recent experiences, I realised that I was more confused than ever about whom I could identify with. Was I capable of maturing into a man, as Ellie had seemed to suggest? Would I instead prefer sleeping with a man myself, if only I could free myself from what was still for me the strange idea of two men kissing? Perhaps I was simply unique, unable to be described by any label, not rigidly fixed in my sexual preferences? I really didn't know.

I hadn't bothered calling on Ellie for several days after she'd turn down my proposal. I was embarrassed to speak with her again, but I knew that our paths would soon cross.

As I was passing her room one evening, I noticed that the door was wide open. I glanced inside and saw that she wasn't around. I made my way into the room, and decided that it would be fun to put myself in Ellie's place. I first sat in her swivel chair, spinning this from side to side, and letting myself feel like a child on a swing.

I then decided to try lying on Ellie's bed, wondering what it might be like were she lying there with me. The bed was small, and not fully to my liking, but in my moment of wild dreaming, this didn't bother me unduly.

As I was rolling my body from side to side and swinging wide my arms, imagining that I was reaching for Ellie, the object of my affections suddenly appeared at the door.

"What are you doing Benny?" she said, firmly but surprisingly calmly. "What are you doing in my room?"

I couldn't offer her an answer, and even wondered myself how I could have been so insolent to have crept into her room.

"I want you out of my room now!" Ellie continued, more assertively now. "Please just go!"

I sheepishly obeyed, muttering that I was sorry as I took my exit.

The following morning, as I was making my way toward the refectory, Grant approached me, making speed toward me and casting a menacing glance. Apart from ourselves, the corridor was empty, and so Grant took the opportunity that he'd been looking for to confront me.

"So you want to be Ellie's new boyfriend, do you, you worthless pratt?" He scowled, gripping my shirt at both epaulets, nearly wrestling me to the ground. "No one comes between Ellie and me, you crappy arsehole!" he continued, now grabbing my arms and shaking me like someone might shake out a rug.

Letting go of me for a moment, allowing both of us to step back and steady ourselves, Grant went on. "So you want a fight, do you big boy?" he goaded me. "Let's see what you're made of, what spunk Ellie's new boyfriend has got inside of him!"

Grant raised his arm, ready to strike me, but I didn't want to fight. I didn't want to get hurt. Gasping and slowly pacing backwards like a coward, I managed to dodge Grant's punch. Quickening my pace, I turned and ran down the corridor as quickly as I could, racing down the stairs to the ground floor, and then making for the exit to the hall. I kept running until I reached Grassmarket, and never returned to the hall again. Grant didn't follow after me.

Afterword

The story of *Goldilocks and the three bears* may have lost some of its original meaning through repeated re-telling. The original story is thought to have cast a she-wolf in the role later played by Goldilocks, which was devoured by the bears on being discovered.

In the modern version of the story, it's not clear where our sympathies should lie. On one hand, Goldilocks seems to want to do little more than to explore and find answers to satisfy her curiosity; on the other, she is an intruder in the bears' home, who seems to show little regard for their property or privacy.

The bears are understandably perturbed when they return home after their walk, but refrain from letting their emotions get the better of them while they look for clues that might identify the intruder. Seeing Little Bear's broken chair and empty bowl, it's possible that the parents suspect that their visitor might still be a child.

Goldilocks is impatient to want to push at doors and try out new things. She does so without regard for others' privacy and property, and without fear of the possible consequences, oblivious to the dangers that she might encounter. Only when her sleep is disturbed does she become afraid, and in her fright, knows no other way of defending herself than to run away. Her golden locks and youthful charm aren't enough alone to win over the bears' favour.

It's perhaps intriguing to wonder what conversation might have ensued had Goldilocks faced up to the bears. Seemingly indifferent to her, it's by no means certain that the parents would have rushed to pounce on her. Perhaps, if she had had a fair explanation for her intrusion, they might even have welcomed her to stay?

Little Bear is the one who suffers the most from Goldilock's interference. His porridge is completely eaten, and his chair is dashed to pieces. It's his screaming that awakens Goldilocks, the screaming of a child who perhaps feels that a new pretender has usurped his place in the family unit.

Hence, there's a possible theme of sibling rivalry that's opened up by the interplay of Goldilock's actions and the concerns of Little Bear. It is he from whom things have been taken, destroyed or seem threatened by a new, older rival.

Goldilocks might also be seen to be on a journey of sexual and self-discovery. She wanders into the depth of an unknown wood, much as a person who seeks to discover themselves needs to venture into their sub-conscious. She makes her journey alone, but in meeting the bears, runs back, looking for the place from which she came. Her growth into sexual maturity or a higher level of self isn't therefore resolved in this story; Goldi-lock's future is left hanging in the balance.

In her testing out the bears' preference for por-ridge, chairs, and beds, Goldilocks explores which identity fits her best. Will it be the cold, hard choice of the father–or perhaps the hot and soft preference of the mother? Goldilocks concludes that it's Little Bear's station that fits her best, but she has already outgrown his chair, and might do better to form an identity that is her own and suitable for her stage in life.

What is clear from the story is that Goldilocks is an outsider. The three bears form a family, each having their own role to play, and each being clear of their relationship to each other. Goldilocks might be at-tracted to join their comfortable household, but she isn't made to feel welcome by them. Ultimately, she knows that she cannot become a part of the bears' family group.

In this story, there's no happy ending. In fact, there's barely an ending at all. It's not clear what effect Goldilock's intrusion has on the bears, while Goldilocks runs away, possibly to get lost in the wood. It may be necessary and right to want to explore, but in order to grow, she–like all of us–must know that it's right to respect others, while learning to face up to the difficult predicaments that we might find ourselves encountering.

Little Red Riding Hood

There once lived a beautiful young girl, whose name was Little Red Riding Hood. She had been given this name because she refused to wear anything other than a riding hood made of red velvet, which had been made for her by her beloved grandmother.

Little Red Riding Hood's grandmother loved her granddaughter so much that she would have given anything for her. Little Red Riding Hood also loved to visit her grandmother, who lived in a small cottage in the middle of the woods.

One day, Little Red Riding Hood's mother asked her daughter if she would like to take a freshly baked pumpkin cake to her grandmother. The poor old lady wasn't feeling well and was too weak to bake a cake for herself.

Little Red Riding Hood was very excited by her mother's suggestion, as this was the first time that she'd been allowed to visit her grandmother all by herself.

"Oh yes mother, please let me go to granny's house!" Little Red Riding Hood eagerly replied. "I will go right away!"

Her mother packed the cake in a small picnic basket, which she covered with a red and white chequered napkin to keep the flies away. Little Red Riding Hood pulled on her long cape and picked up the basket.

"My dear, do be careful!" said her mother, as Little Red Riding Hood stood by the door. "Do not speak to anyone that you don't know and go quickly to granny's house, staying on the path that you know at all times."

"I'll go quickly, dear mother, I promise!" said Little Red Riding Hood, "I won't stop until I come to granny's house."

With that, she kissed her mother goodbye and skipped off in the direction of her grandmother's cottage.

Shortly along the path, not long after she'd entered the woods, she came across a wolf, who was passing by. Not yet knowing that wolves can be devious and dangerous creatures, Little Red Riding Hood was not at all afraid to meet this kindly looking stranger.

"Good morning Mr. Wolf!" Little Red Riding Hood joyfully cried. "My name is Little Red Riding Hood and

I'm taking a freshly baked cake to my grandmother, who is unwell."

"I'm very pleased to meet you," said the wolf. "How sad to hear that your grandmother is unwell. Perhaps if you let me know where she lives, I might also drop by to see her when I am passing by that way?"

"I think she would like that very much," said Little Red Riding Hood. "To walk to her house takes fifteen minutes further along the path, where you'll see it nestling between three large oak trees."

"I will pass by that way later," said the wolf, "and will bid your grandmother my good wishes."

"You are very kind," said Little Red Riding Hood.

All along, the wolf was thinking to himself, "What a beautiful, tender young creature this Little Red Riding Hood is! I would very much like to eat her! Maybe if I'm clever, I will be able to eat her grandmother too. That will really satisfy my hungry belly!"

The wolf also knew that he would not be able to eat Little Red Riding Hood right away, as there were woodcutters working close by who would surely hear her scream.

Suddenly, the wolf had an idea.

"Look at those beautiful flowers," he said to Little Red Riding Hood, pointing to the many flowers growing alongside the path. "Maybe you might pick some as a present for your grandmother, to take along together with your delicious cake?"

"Oh what a good idea!" said Little Red Riding Hood, "It will only take me a moment to pick a few and granny will be very pleased to have them!"

Forgetting her mother's warning, Little Red Riding Hood gaily stepped off the path to where the flowers were growing. "I will gather a small posy," she thought to herself.

The sun's rays sparkled on the carpet of flowers around her like the bright beams of a star light up the night sky. Birds sang cheerfully in the nearby trees. Bright-eyed rabbits hopped from one little clump of flowers to another. A gentle trickle of water flowing in a nearby stream added its refreshing echo to the melody of simple sounds in the forest. It was very beautiful.

Little Red Riding Hood was enraptured by the beauty, and started to wander further and further from the path to gather more and more beautiful flowers.

Meanwhile, the wolf had run further along the path toward grandmother's house.

"Ha, Ha!" He said himself, "That foolish girl has fallen for my cunning plan!"

When he arrived at grandmother's house, the wolf knocked on the door three times.

"Who's that?" came grandmother's faint cry.

"It is I, Little Red Riding Hood," said the wolf, trying to disguise his voice as best he could. "I have brought you a delicious cake to eat."

"Come in my dear," answered grandmother, "I am too weak to leave my bed to open the door."

The wolf went straight to grandmother's bedroom, but rather than giving her the cake, which he rather fancied himself, without a word, he pounced on grandmother and swallowed her up in a single gulp!

Aware that Little Red Riding Hood might arrive at any moment, the wolf slipped on grandmother's nightdress and nightcap and jumped straight into her bed.

Meanwhile, back in the woods, Little Red Riding Hood suddenly remembered her mother's advice that she should stay on the path. Having gathered a beautiful posy of flowers, she found her way back to where she had met the wolf and then skipped merrily along the path toward her grandmother's cottage.

When she arrived, Little Red Riding Hood was surprised to see that the door was open. She knocked on the door three times, but there came no reply.

"Granny are you there?" asked Little Red Riding Hood. Still no reply came.

"Something doesn't feel quite right," Little Red Riding Hood thought to herself. "I don't feel quite as comfortable as I normally do when visiting granny's house."

Little Red Riding Hood couldn't work out why she might feel this way, but she stepped into the house, going straight to her grandmother's bedroom.

There, Little Red Riding Hood saw her grandmother lying in the bed, but she didn't look like quite
like she did normally. "Maybe granny is more unwell
than I realized!" thought Little Red Riding Hood.

Seeing her grandmother's strangely big ears sticking out of her nightcap, Little Red Riding Hood exclaimed, "Oh grandmother, what big ears you have!"

"All the better to hear you with, my dear!" came the
faint reply.

"Oh grandmother, what big eyes you have!"
shrieked Little Red Riding Hood, seeing two huge bulging eyes peeping out from underneath the bedclothes.

"All the better to see you with, my dear!" came the
reply. "But come closer, my dear, so that I might give
you a hug."

The wolf stretched out an arm to embrace Little
Red Riding Hood, but it was much bigger and much
furrier than she remembered. Startled, Little Red Riding Hood could only exclaim, "Oh grandmother, what
big arms you have!"

"All the better to hug you with!" answered the wolf.

Little Red Riding Hood snuggled up on the bed
alongside the wolf, resting her head on his broad chest,
breathing in time with the ups and downs of his body.
For a moment, she felt safe and warm in the caress of
his large arm.

Little Red Riding Hood turned her head to kiss her
grandmother, but then noticed that she had a much

larger mouth and longer protruding teeth than she remembered before. The poor, confused child cried, "Grandmother, what big teeth you have!"

"All the better to eat you with!" came the wolf's very sudden and very loud reply.

At this, the wolf leapt out of the bed in a single bound and swallowed Little Red Riding Hood right up whole—in just one gulp!

"Oh I feel well satisfied now!" said the wolf contentedly to himself. "And there's still a delicious cake waiting for my tea!"

With his belly full and after the adventures of the day, the wolf suddenly felt very tired. Climbing back into grandmother's bed, he quickly fell into a deep sleep and before long was snoring very loudly.

It happened that a huntsman was passing close by the little house at the time, looking for wolves to kill. He knew grandmother well and, hearing the loud snoring, thought to himself that he should stop by to see if she needed anything that he might be able to bring to her.

Seeing that the door to the little house was open and hearing that its occupant was still sleeping, he quietly stepped into the house and tiptoed very gently to grandmother's bedroom.

When he entered the room, he immediately saw that it was the wolf who was snoring loudly, and he guessed that the poor grandmother had been eaten by the wolf!

"I've been looking for you, you old thief!" muttered the huntsman, a smile growing on his face as he began to realize that this was his lucky day.

Taking his gun, the huntsman was about to shoot the wolf when he thought better of it, telling himself, "Maybe grandmother might still be alive inside the wolf's belly. If I'm very careful, perhaps she might still be saved."

So he put down his gun and instead took a pair of scissors, which he used to very gently cut open the wolf's stomach.

No sooner had he done this than out popped Little Red Riding Hood.

"Thank you Mr. Huntsman for saving me!" said Little Red Riding Hood, "It was so horribly dark in there! I was so afraid and didn't know whether I might ever be free."

The huntsman was surprised to see Little Red Riding Hood, but her grandmother had also just been able to breathe inside the wolf's tummy, and she then stepped out right behind her granddaughter.

"While the wolf is still sleeping," said the huntsman, "Perhaps we can gather some stones to fill his belly with, and then sew his skin together again?"

Little Red Riding Hood rushed off to collect some stones and did as the huntsman said.

When the wolf awoke, he felt very ill. The weight of the stones made him feel very heavy and he struggled to breathe. Seeing that Little Red Riding Hood and her grandmother had escaped, and gazing at the huntsman–who was staring straight in his eyes–the wolf realized that there was no escape for him. With one exhausted sigh, he collapsed and stopped breathing.

The huntsman lopped off the wolf's head and cut open his skin, which he planned to turn into a rug.

Finally, Little Red Riding Hood was able to give her grandmother the cake that she had brought from her mother, along with the posy of flowers that she had collected in the woods.

"Oh my dear, how good it is that you are safe!" said her grandmother. "Now we will enjoy tea and cake together!"

Little Red Riding Hood was very grateful to the huntsman and pleased to be safe with her grandmother again. But she said to herself, "Never again will I forget my mother's warning not to speak to strangers and to keep to the path that I know!"

Little Red Riding Hood made sure that she went straight home when she left her grandmother's house that day. "I'm going to listen very carefully to what mother tells me," she thought to herself. And that's exactly what she did from that day on.

Summer with Rosie

Note: This chapter includes a depiction of sexual assault that may be disturbing for some readers.

Summer holidays aren't meant to be like this. End-less rain. Ever-lingering gray clouds. England getting kicked out of the rugby in the first round. I want to be out with my mates, but that's not going to happen right now.

Mum says that she doesn't want me to go out alone. My mates come round here, but they don't know what to say to me. My counsellor tells me to give myself time. *Time?* I never knew how long the hours can be until I was sitting here in my room, as I am now. My mind just can't stop turning over what's happened. I feel empty, dirty, confused. At times I can do nothing but cry, but my tears just seep away into the duvet.

I'll be going back to school in a few weeks when the holiday is over, at least if my psychiatrist says that I'm well enough to. I can't wait to get back to normal life again, if life ever can be normal again after what I've been through.

I suppose my experience is no different from many others'. You just have to look at how busy they are at the centre where I go for counselling. The place is running flat out working with people like me. "Rosie," they say, "You're unique, you're special. You matter." But I know that they're just trying to be kind. There are hundreds like me that pass through their doors, perhaps even thousands.

I've been stupid, I know that. Well perhaps not stupid, but at least bloody naive. Mum had told me about Pete, my aunt Miriam's boyfriend, long ago.

"He's not all he seems, my girl," she warned me. "Nice enough on the outside, but don't you go thinking that he's getting you all these treats for nothing." Of course I didn't pay any attention to her, nor, if I'm honest, would I have known at the time what she meant if I had.

Pete had seemed a nice enough chap. I'd known him for at least four years now, since he moved in with my aunt. I'd been going to her house every evening after school because my mum was still working. Aunty

Miriam used to make my tea and drop me off at mum's before starting her nightshift at the South Bristol Community Hospital, not far from where we lived in the Hengrove area of Bristol.

My aunt had always done everything for me. She washed my gym kit, cut my hair, made my tea. I think that she would have done anything for me if she could. Still would, but now that the Huntington's disease is taking a hold on her, she's spending more and more time in hospital. That's where she was when what happened happened.

I know that my mum worries sick about me. She's had almost all of her holiday time off from work these past few weeks just to look after me. But she needs to work, especially since my dad left us when I was still at junior school and doesn't pay his share of the maintenance.

Pete–"Uncle Pete" as I've called him since I've known him–did odd jobs around the Avonmouth Docks. Sometimes he worked nights just like my aunt– sometimes just a few days here, or even just a day– wherever he could get a contract. I never knew quite what he was doing, but he seemed to bring in some money, enough to buy things for my aunt.

In fact, as far as I can see, he was pretty generous to her. However, my mum saw things differently, saying that he didn't really love her, but wanted to marry her so that he could then divorce her soon after, and then get half of her money. I really don't know the truth, but my mum's no bad judge of character.

My aunt worked hard. Nurses always do. She didn't like the way things were going at the hospital, but she had a job and liked to think that she was helping people.

She liked to be treated by Pete once in awhile. He took her to the pictures at *Cineworld*, to *Smiley's Plaice* in Bedminster–the best chippy restaurant this side of the Avon–and every Thursday, to the *Gala Bingo* at Hengrove Park. They'd scooped the £100 prize there once in awhile, but goodness knows how much they'd had to spend in the process.

I suppose my aunt is beginning to feel her age, especially since her health problems have kicked in. She's a lot older than my mum and had been more like a mother to her when they were young. Now she likes to know what I think about clothes and what looks I fancy. She bought me a black leather biker's jacket from *FCUK* for my thirteenth birthday, and when I don't have to wear school uniform, this is always my favourite jacket to go out in.

Pete often bought me things too. At least I think he bought them–I never asked where they came from. It was very handy for keeping in with what my mates had at school–an S5 Galaxy phone, a new pair of Adidas trainers, even a second-hand iPad. I just had to ask, and Pete would provide.

He took me out for a bite from time to time too, to the Frankie and Benny's at Hengrove Park, and sometimes with my aunt to *Smiley's Plaice*. Pete was always very chatty when my aunt was around, quite a comedian at times.

But I can see now that Pete didn't just want to be a likeable uncle. That's why I'm in this mess right now. Let me take you back just three brief weeks to that awful afternoon, an afternoon that I've replayed in my mind probably a thousand times.

I suppose, from what I've said, it doesn't take a genius to work out that Uncle Pete and I got into an intimate situation. Grooming, assault, rape...I don't know what you'd call it; sometimes these things are difficult to pin down.

Doubtless, the prosecution will have their view when this goes to trial. That's one more moment in the future that I want to banish from my mind right now. Mum says that if nothing else, they'll do him for having sex with someone who's below the age of consent. But I'm fourteen, for heaven's sake, and capable of looking after myself. At least I thought I was.

The school holiday had just started. Six weeks freedom from the Oasis Academy John Williams and Mr. Quinn's tedious maths lessons. Mum had booked a week off from work, and we were going to stay with her other sister, who lives just outside of Scarborough. Better still, Justin Bieber was playing at the O2, and I was going to see him with one of my mates and her dad.

Pete was going through one of his "off" periods between contracts and so was spending a lot of time at my aunt's place. Because my mum was out working during the day, I used to hang out at their house most of the time when I was off from school. Pete was generally good company, and before my aunt went in to the South Bristol, she was generally a laugh to be around too.

For this holiday, it was just Pete and me. We kept out of each others' way most of the time—me Facebooking my mates, and Pete making sparks fly on his Xbox. He'd break from time to time to pop his head around the spare bedroom door, which was my second home. "Want a cuppa, princess?" he'd say, or, "Just nipping out for a bit to see your aunt. There's a cheese and pickle sarnie waiting for you in the fridge..."

I went out a bit as well. Most days I went to visit my aunt at the hospital, usually with Pete before he dropped me off at my mum's. I also spent some time hanging around with my mates at *Frankie and Benny's*, but most of the time I was quite happy sitting in front of the computer at my aunt's.

By the end of the first week of the holiday, Pete and I were starting to get into some interesting conversations. He'd taken it upon himself to play his uncle role with real dedication, and I enjoyed our lively banter.

One afternoon, we got talking about relationships. I suppose he thought that I was old enough to get into talking about such stuff. One or two of my mates already had boyfriends. I'd seen some of them kissing and snogging down at the skate park, and I confided this to Pete.

"Do you think they're really in love?" I asked him.

"Puppy love is what they call that, princess," was his reply. "I'm not knocking it, we all go through that phase. It's quite innocent when a girl and a fella first start hanging out together. Those first tender kisses...the touch of her breath on your face...feeling her newly-shaped breasts pressing against your chest...magic!"

I had been feeling the changes in my own body for sometime. For me, homework had taken priority over getting a boyfriend, and there was no one quite like Justin Bieber that I'd yet come across at my school. But what the world hadn't yet provided, my imagination did a pretty good job of filling in.

Lying on my bed, strange and wonderful urges tantalising my body, I dreamt of being felt by a real–I mean *fully* adult–man. Not a babe in arms like those puppy lovers, but feeling the strong, warm, electrifying touch on my exposed, sensitive flesh. I wanted to be properly held, to feel protected and loved. I wanted to experience the magic of being touched, to taste the rich texture of a lover's tongue, and maybe–yes,

maybe–to welcome the solid thrust of his manhood secretly venturing deeper into the warm interior of my
body.

"Uncle Pete," I mumbled. "How can I find a boyfriend who can show me, you know, what goes on between a real man and a woman...not the puppy love
stuff that my mates brag about?"

"You'll get to know all about that soon enough,
princess," Pete replied. "There's plenty of time before
you need to worry about that just yet. Get yourself a
boyfriend when you're ready, and just take one step at
a time. That's what I would do if I could do it all
again."

Maybe my urges were getting the better of me,
maybe it was just curiosity, but I decided then and
there that I didn't want to spend years just fantasising
about what it would be like to be with a man, even if
my fantasy could come real just once.

Not wanting to let the subject go, I hesitated before
posing my next question, but it just came out anyhow,
without a trace of nervousness. "Would you show me
what it feels like to be touched?" I asked.

I don't even know where this idea came from–until
then, I'd not really seen Pete as anything other than
my "uncle". But in fairness, he wasn't too bad looking,
being a good fifteen years younger than my aunt.

"I couldn't, princess," he replied. "It wouldn't be right. Besides, young lady, you're still much younger than you think!"

"I'm not that young, Uncle Pete," I retorted. "I only want to know what it's like to be touched, to be held."

"Sorry, princess, no!" Pete repeated. He seemed to be insistent, and quickly changed the subject.

I went back to the book that I was reading, but could hardly focus on the words. My mind had woken up to the wild possibility of being taught a lesson or two in love by my very own Uncle Pete! Nothing too unseemly, mind you, just a little foray into the world of adult life.

Nothing more was said on the matter that day. We visited my aunt at the hospital as usual, then Pete dropped me off at my mum's. But just before seeing me up my mother's path, Pete did something that he hadn't done before. Bending down a little to reach my height, he threw a gentle hug around my shoulders and then kissed me fully on the lips. "Night, night, princess," he whispered. "Sweet dreams!"

I don't really know what people mean when they say that they are in ecstasy, but I thought that I might just have found out. I said nothing to my mum, heading straight to my room, where I threw myself on my bed and gazed at the poster of Justin Bieber that was hanging on the wall. "Are you a real man too, dear Justin?" I

mused. But my most favourite person of all time didn't
answer. He never did.

ક્ર•ર્જી

"Rosie, the toast is getting cold!" shouted my
mother. "I've got to go to work now, it's already half-
past-eight." I must have slept well, still not quite regis-
tering where I was. I was in no rush to get up, but the
sun was already in full ascent and I'd promised Pete
that I would be at my aunt's by ten.

My curtains still drawn, I threw back the duvet,
slipped off my nightdress and made my first steps of
the day around the room, positioning myself so that I
could see my whole body reflected in the wardrobe's
full-length mirror. I was well familiar with the contours of my face, having spent hours in front of the
bathroom mirror, plastering it with moisturising
cream and skin cleansing gels. But I rarely took a good
look at all of me.

"You're not that bad looking, girl!" I prided myself.
"You've come quite a long way since leaving Perry
Court Junior!"

My breasts were forming nicely. So much so, that
I'd had my first bra fitted at Debenhams when I was
only thirteen. The dark brown curls of my hair
brushed gently over my soft shoulder blades. I had
some way to go before getting an hourglass hipline, but
the distinctive curves of a young woman's body were
obvious. I ran my hand over my right breast, absorbing

its warmth. Closing my eyes, I rooted myself in the moment. Cupping my hands over my mouth to deflect my breath, I imagined that my cheeks were being caressed by the strong exhalation of a man. Perhaps it might have been Pete.

I didn't allow myself to indulge in moments like this very often, but I resolved that I wouldn't shy away from embracing my blossoming sexuality any longer.

After washing and dressing, I quickly downed the tea and toast that my mum had left me, and set off for my aunt's house.

On arrival, I was surprised to see that Pete wasn't around. He'd left a note on the kitchen table, which explained that he'd had to go into town unexpectedly. I assumed that he'd been called for an interview over at the docks. I only found out later that he'd in fact dropped by the hospital to make sure that my aunt wasn't going to be coming home any time soon.

Pete got home in time for lunch, a quick microwaved pizza from Sainsbury's. As we munched on our pepperoni slices, Pete seemed to be looking at me more intently than normal, having what looked like quite a devilish glint in his eyes.

I too felt somehow more in touch with him than I could remember being before, almost as though we had a shared secret that went beyond that kiss.

"Uncle Pete," I started, "Thank you for that lovely kiss last night. I've hardly stopped thinking about it."

"You're welcome, princess," he replied, taking a bite off a stick of celery, picked off from the side salad that had come with our pizza.

"You know, I've been thinking," he continued, "Maybe it wouldn't be so wrong for me to show you a thing or two about what us grown-up's get up to when the light's switched off. Nothing over the top, mind you. You're not my real niece after all, even though I treat you like my own flesh and blood. I wish I'd been shown a trick or two when I was fourteen by someone I could trust."

"What do you have in mind?" I asked, conscious that my excitement over his suggestion must have been obvious to him.

"Only what you're ready for, princess," he promised. "And only if you want to."

He cut away the crust of a fresh slice of pizza, seeming to be wholly absorbed in his task before staring at me straight in the eyes and continuing, "We could start with me undressing you, very slowly, and seeing where we go from there?"

"I would like that very much," I replied without hesitating, almost stumbling over my words in my urgency to pin him down to his word.

We finished lunch, and I started to clear the dishes, as I always did.

"Leave the dishes, Rosie!" Pete interrupted. "You go and prepare yourself in your aunt's bedroom. I'll come up to you in just a few moments."

I didn't quite know what he meant when he spoke about preparing myself, but I simply sat on my aunt's dressing table chair, swivelling it from side to side as I slipped off my slippers, straightened my hair, and anticipated Pete's entrance in the bedroom. I'd been in my aunt's bedroom several times before, but never with a feeling like I had now.

Pete entered the room and stood behind me. He placed his hands gently on my shoulders and crouched down so that he could press his cheek against mine. We both stared at the dressing table mirror in front of us.

"Are you ready, you beautiful woman?" he whispered directly into my ear.

I felt a tear fall down my left cheek, my heart was racing. I simply looked at him expectantly and smiled.

Pete allowed his hands to run gently down the full length of both my arms then stood up again to turn the seat on which I was sitting, before reaching for my right hand and beckoning me to follow him to stand close by the side of the bed.

"Are you sure that you're comfortable with this?" repeated Pete.

"I've never been surer," I unhesitatingly replied.

Pete stroked my hair, allowing my curls to separate between his fingers. He placed his right arm around me and kissed me, straight on the mouth. I felt that I wanted the kiss to deepen and quite instinctively found my tongue inviting contact with his. Pete's tongue did all that it could to entwine with mine.

We kissed like this for perhaps several minutes, I do not know for how long, before Pete gently removed his tongue from my mouth and again asked me how I felt.

Without speaking, I motioned for him to undress me.

Pete stroked my head, then traced his hand along the delicate curve of my spine.

"Let me help you to loosen up," he whispered, unfastening the button on my chinos. He gently opened the zip to its full extent, and then, with both hands, peeled the snugly fitting pants away from my skin. He allowed his hands to rest on my buttocks for a moment before letting the jeans drop to the floor.

He then rested on his knees and peeled off each of my striped "happy" socks. As he did so, he let his hand run over the soles of my feet and played with each toe, squeezing each in turn between his finger and his thumb.

Rising to his feet again, Pete stood for a while, outstretching his arms to gently grip mine. He stared keenly into my eyes.

"You're beautiful," he said simply. I believed he was being sincere. He kissed me on the neck, and then proceeded to unbutton my blouse, from my collar button to my waist. Very gently, he then unhooked the sleeves of the blouse from my shoulders, allowing the soft wrapping of cotton to fall quickly from my arms.

"Step forward a little, my darling," beckoned Pete. He motioned me to face the wardrobe's mirror. Now I was wearing nothing except my bra and panties. "Are you still sure you want me to continue?" Pete again enquired. "Yes," I repeated, as though automatically.

Pete stood behind me, so that we could both see my reflection in the full-length mirror. He unfastened my bra, and I held out my arms in front of me to allow the straps to fall away from me. Then he crouched behind me and gently pulled down my panties, letting these fall to the floor, where I could easily completely free myself from them.

We stood together for a moment, just staring in the mirror—my fully naked body on show before Pete, Pete still fully clothed. I felt a strange mix of vulnerability and safety, but was also aware of enjoying my own beauty and the excitement of the moment.

Pete proceeded to take off his own clothes, but did not offer me the same opportunity to admire his body. Instead, he pulled back the duvet of my aunt's bed and invited me to lay in the very spot where she normally slept. I unhesitatingly obeyed, waiting for Pete to crawl in beside me. He climbed alongside and just held my hand for a moment or two, as we both stared at the ceiling, without speaking. I might have been staring at the whole Universe in that moment. It was just magical.

After a brief time, Pete released his hand, turned to look at me and whispered, "Do you want me to go further?" His words were paced almost as though he didn't really intend to ask the question, but I'd already decided upon my answer anyway.

"Please touch me...touch me. I want to be touched!" I cried.

Pete rolled onto his side and then moved into a cat stretch over the top of me. I found my legs widening, my thighs making contact with his. He then gently relaxed from his hovering position to hold me in a firm caress, his head resting next to mine. I felt our hearts beating, our breath caressing each other's skin, and shuddered with the wet pleasure of Pete's kiss, as he started to navigate his lips all over my tender skin.

Pete's hands moved slowly but firmly as he traced the contours of my body. The slow glide of his hands over my breasts brought a sensation much more powerful than I'd imagined in my fantasies. Our mouths again found contact and our tongues twisted and turned as we explored each other's inner anatomies.

Pete's hand moved from stroking my hair to squeezing my buttocks. And then, between the kisses, he calmly asked me, "Do you want me to go still further?"

I cannot honestly remember whether I replied or not. All I remember is being lost in that moment, not aware of anything other than Pete's strong presence. And so he allowed his very firm penis to find its way into my most sacred place.

I hadn't expected to feel so uneasy at this, but it was my first time and Pete was a very strong man. I let out what I thought was a small scream, but what Pete alleges was just a normal groan. He kept coming.

The magic of the moment earlier was quickly replaced with terror as I realized my helplessness. But Pete kept whispering, "Relax, this is what it's like for everyone their first time. You're beautiful, we're beautiful," and other such things.

It was over quite suddenly. He withdrew from my body, stroked my left cheek and planted a kiss on the other, before saying, "I think we've gone far enough for one day, princess, don't you?"

Pete washed, dressed and disappeared off into the lounge, seemingly as though nothing had happened. I could barely move, unable to comprehend what had happened to me. All the wonder and excitement that I'd felt earlier in the day was gone. I simply felt abused, guilty and ashamed.

Once I could collect myself, I slipped out of my aunt's house while Pete was screaming at his Xbox, and ran back to my mum's as fast as I could. She heard me crying in my room when she got home from work. I told her everything that had happened.

Pete was arrested and taken in for questioning. He was charged the next day with sexual assault of a minor. He's already appeared at Bristol Magistrates' Court to confirm his identity, and is now out on bail, but he isn't allowed to have any contact with me.

The counselling is helping, but they say that it's going to be a long time before I get over this. I feel determined to come through. I've got exams at school to think about, and I don't want to cause my mum and my aunt any more worry.

Strangely, my dad's appeared back on the scene since all this happened. We'd barely heard from him for several years since he went off with another woman, but my mum thought that it was right that he should know what had happened. He's brought me presents and seems to want to spend a lot of time with me, making up for the lost years.

Mum too is very worried about me and says that she is thinking of giving up work, but I don't want her to have to go on benefits. I don't know whether I'll be going back to my aunt's when the school holiday is over. One thing that's for sure—nothing is ever going to be the same again.

Afterword

Numerous versions of the *Little Red Riding Hood* tale have been written. The Grimm brothers alone produced two versions, both with happier endings than the earlier telling by Perrault, in which both the child and her grandmother don't survive being swallowed by the wolf.

The story obviously highlights Little Red Riding Hood's naivety and blind trusting of others, albeit going against her mother's warnings. As so often happens in real life, she learns the hard way, and becomes dependent on others to rescue her from the predicament that she falls into.

Commentators on the story usually refer to the undertext of Little Red Riding Hood's emerging sexuality, pointing out that while she is curious and easily tempted, she lacks the maturity to take on the adult world. Of course, she also wears red–a colour that's often associated with intense passion.

The wolf is able to out-think her and out-manoeuvre her, while avoiding the risk of falling into trouble himself when he is within earshot of the woodcutters in the wood. He is an accomplished thief, a brilliant schemer and the perfect charmer. Like many, he is ready to seize an opportunity if he thinks he can get away with his wicked way, even if this means seriously

abusing someone who's much younger and more vulnerable than himself.

The old and infirm grandmother is incapable of
protecting herself, let alone her granddaughter. This
task is left rightly to Little Red Riding Hood's mother,
who while not on the scene for most the time, fully
understands her daughter's tendency to stray from safe
paths. She ultimately becomes her confidante when the
child realizes that her mother usually does know best.

It's another male figure who acts as rescuer in the
form of the huntsman, contrasting with the animalistic
predatory impulses of the wolf.

In the Grimm brothers' versions of the tale, Little
Red Riding Hood, along with her grandmother, are
brought back to life–reborn, as it were, perhaps more
aware of the risks of giving in to the temptation of
trusting anyone in the worlds that they inhabit. There
might then be hope for those who follow her example–
that a rebirthing might offer a rite of passage into a
more grounded adolescence.

Jack and the beanstalk

During the days of King Arthur there lived a poor woman, whose tiny cottage was far from the city. She had long been a widow and had borne only one son, whom she doted on constantly.

Her son's name was Jack, and he was a lazy boy. Jack rarely thanked his mother for the many kindnesses that she showed to him, and thought that it was his right to be fed and served by her.

Despite his ungratefulness, Jack's mother didn't reproach him, but continued to spoil him in every way that she could.

One day, however, the poor widow had nothing more to give to Jack. He had indulged all that she had, and now they were close to starving.

"Oh you greedy boy!" Jack's mother finally complained. "I've given you all that I have, but you've never shown me any gratitude! Now we have nothing–not even food for us to eat!"

Jack felt ashamed for a moment, but soon put aside what his mother had said.

All that remained of his mother's possessions was her beloved cow. "I do not wish to see my beautiful cow sold," Jack's mother cried, "But I don't know what else we can do!"

Thinking that his mother would never allow him to carry out her threat, Jack teased his mother, saying that he would take the cow to market the very next day. In desperation, Jack's mother agreed, and so he set off on his way to the village early the next morning, leading the cow behind him.

Along the way, Jack happened upon a butcher, who was also making his way to the village. The butcher asked Jack where he was going, and Jack told him the reason for his journey.

Now the butcher was a crafty man, and never gave up an opportunity to make himself a good deal when he saw one. He asked Jack what price he wanted for the cow, and offered to give Jack a collection of small beans that he carried under his hat as a part of the bargain.

Jack was overjoyed with what he thought was a princely offering, and swiftly made the deal with the butcher, exchanging his cow for a small pittance and a handful of beans.

Racing home to tell his mother of their supposed good fortune, Jack exclaimed, "Oh my dear mother, look what I've brought for us in exchange for the cow!"

Seeing the tiny collection of beans, Jack's mother screamed and made so as to beat her son. "Oh you foolish boy, what have you done?" she cried, grabbing at the beans and throwing them all around. Jack was sent to his room, and both he and his mother went without supper that night.

When morning came, Jack was astonished to see that a very tall beanstalk had taken root outside the cottage, where some of the scattered seeds had landed. In no time at all, the beanstalk had grown to a great height. Its mighty stalk was thicker than the trunk of an oak tree! In fact, its body was made up of two giant stalks, which had twisted around each other in such a way as to create a sturdy ladder.

Jack could not believe his eyes. Looking up into the sky, he couldn't see where the giant plant ended. Its crown was high above the clouds.

"I must journey up this magical plant," Jack thought to himself. "Perhaps there will be treasure at the top." He tested his footing on the ladder formed by the tree's giant stalks, seeing that it would easily support his weight.

Firm in his resolution to climb the great tree, Jack presented his plan to his mother. She was at great pains to deter him from his ambition, but he was determined, and disobeyed her wishes.

Early the next morning, Jack set about his long climb. It took many hours before he reached above the clouds, and then finally he came to the place where the beanstalk reached its full height.

Jack looked around, and saw before him what looked like a desert landscape—a barren land strewn with rough stones and occasional clumps of grass. Exhausted from his climb, Jack sat down on one of the large stones, wondering what he might do next.

No sooner had he done this, than there appeared a young woman in the distance, making toward Jack. When she arrived where Jack was sitting, he noticed that she carried a white wand in her hand, which was capped with a golden peacock. Jack explained to the woman how he had come to this strange land.

He said that he was sorry that he had left his mother behind, going against her wishes. The young woman then asked Jack to talk about his father, but Jack knew nothing about him.

"My mother has never told me anything about my father," Jack explained to the woman. "I have asked her many times to tell me of him, but she is always very troubled when I raise such questions, and refuses to say anything about him."

"I can reveal the secret that your mother is hiding from you," the young woman replied. "I am a fairy, and was the guardian for your father until the day he died."

The fairy went on to relate the full detail of what had happened. "Your father was a very good man, generous to everyone that he met, but especially to the poor. He was himself wealthy, and he frequently opened his home to those who were starving and suffering."

Jack listened in awe as the fairy continued, "The kindness of a man such as this soon became widely known, and so it was that a giant who lived many miles away came to hear about your father's benevolence. The giant was as evil in his manner as your father was kind, and he wished to acquire your father's riches for himself.

"Travelling to your father's house, the evil giant made out that he and his wife had escaped with their lives, following an earthquake in the neighbourhood where they lived. Your father immediately took pity on them, and promised to take them into his house, offering them fine meals, and affording them comfortable accommodation.

"The giant eagerly accepted your father's generous hospitality," the fairy went on, "But he desired to have everything that his host possessed. One day, he recognised an opportunity that might allow him to fulfil his evil wish.

"Looking out far over the horizon through the lens of a telescope, the giant espied a crew of mariners, whose ship had come to grief upon a rock. Rushing to your father, the giant related what he had seen, and proposed that your father send all of his servants to help rescue the troubled crew.

"Your father naturally agreed, and immediately dispatched all of those who served him, save for his porter and the nurse. While the servants were gone, the giant joined your father in his study, where he was reading. Your father suggested a book that the giant may like to read, and climbed onto his library steps to fetch the book from a shelf.

"As he was doing so," the fairy continued, her voice now trembling, "The evil giant rushed behind your father, and stabbed him in the back with a knife. He left the body lying in the study, and then proceeded to dispatch the porter and the nurse, fearing that they might have been witnesses to his crime.

"Your mother was nursing you in a distant room of the house. You were only three weeks old at the time."

At this point, the fairy started crying, taking a moment to collect herself before continuing her story. "I was not able to help your father when the giant struck," she went on, "As my powers had been temporally suspended, because I had erred against the fairies' bond. My punishment was only ended once your father had fallen to the floor."

Jack could barely believe what he was hearing, but begged the fairy to go on. "The giant would have taken your mother and you too in an instant," she continued, "But your mother threw herself at his feet, and begged that he spared your lives. In a moment, the giant was suddenly filled with remorse, and he granted that you and your mother could escape from the house–but only on condition that she swore never to tell you anything about your father.

"Your mother hurried quickly from the house, bearing you in her arms. She travelled many miles before resting, fearing that the giant might come after her. Finally, she settled at the place where your cottage now stands."

Jack wondered what might have happened to the giant when his father's servants returned from their expedition. The fairy soon answered the question that was running through his mind. "The giant knew that he must act quickly before the servants returned," she continued. "He gathered all of your father's finest treasures, and then started fires in different rooms of the mansion. When the servants returned, the giant was gone, and the house was a smouldering ruin."

"The mercy that the giant had shown in allowing you and your mother to escape lasted no more than a moment, and soon he reverted to his evil nature." The fairy paused for a moment, before continuing. "It was I who gave you protection when your mother fled the house, and I too that inspired you to exchange your cow for the handful of magical beans. The beanstalk grew so strongly and so quickly because of my power, and your great desire to climb it was also kindled by my design."

"You have come to the land where the giant resides," said the fairy. "You are the person that must kill the giant to avenge your father's death, and recapture as many of the treasures that he stole as you can, for they are rightfully yours. I warn you, you will face many dangers in your quest, but you must persevere, or forever live a life of misery. If you do as I say, I will always protect you. Follow now the straight path that you see before you to the mansion on the other side of the hill. That is where you will find the giant."

At this, the fairy disappeared, leaving Jack to contemplate the terrifying challenge that now confronted him. Tired and hungry, Jack made quickly for the giant's mansion, hoping that he might be able to beg for food, and possibly find a place to rest his body.

Arriving at the mansion, Jack met a woman, who was standing by the door.

"Who is this that comes to our door?" the woman asked, seeming surprised to see Jack. "We do not see many people coming near here," continued the woman, "For it is well-known that my husband likes nothing more than to eat flesh of the human kind. He thinks nothing of travelling many miles to search for his favourite dish!"

Jack was terrified at what the woman told him, but remembering the fairy's promise to protect him, he replied, "Dear lady, I am a poor traveller, desperate for food, and looking for a place to rest my weary head for the night. Please will you allow me entry into your home?"

The woman repeated her warning about the giant, imploring Jack not to stay near this place of great danger. But Jack was determined, and finally the woman agreed to bid him entry.

She led Jack through many grand rooms, filled with wonderful treasures. Following through a long gallery, Jack heard the wailing of men, coming from what he assumed was a dungeon.

"What is that loud wailing that I can hear?" he asked the woman.

"Those are the cries of the men that my husband has captured, awaiting their time to be served for his supper."

Hearing this, Jack was most terrified. He even began to distrust the woman that had taken him in, fearing that she might lead him to the same dungeon from which he heard the men's howling. He felt that his life might nearly be over, but still he remembered the fairy's instruction to persevere.

The woman brought Jack into a giant kitchen. A healthy fire was crackling in the hearth. Jack could see a large chair, and a gigantic table. The woman invited Jack to take a seat, and offered him food and drink, which he quickly consumed.

No sooner had he finished his meal, than Jack heard what sounded like an elephants' stampede approaching the house. "My husband is returning!" the woman quickly cried. "Quick, you must hide in the oven, lest he sees you!"

The woman bundled Jack into the oven, which fortunately she hadn't yet made ready for cooking. Here, Jack cowered behind a tiny grille, through which he could see the giant berating his wife.

"Fi, Fi, Fo, Fum! I smell the blood of an Englishman!" hollered the giant.

"No, my dear husband," the woman frantically tried to reassure him. "There is no fresh blood here, only that of the men who are awaiting my master's pleasure in the dungeon."

Jack realised now that the woman could be trusted, and he reeled when he saw the cruel manner with which the ogre bellowed at his wife.

"Woman, bring me my supper!" the giant demanded, and his wife faithfully set about preparing his meal.

Jack was astonished to see how much food the giant devoured. When his appetite seemed satisfied, the giant ordered his wife to bring him his hen, such that he might amuse himself.

The woman brought out the most beautiful hen, which was placed on the table in front of the giant.

"Lay!" the giant ordered. No sooner had the word left his mouth, than the hen laid a solid gold egg. She repeated to lay eggs whenever the giant commanded her.

After a time, the giant fell asleep in front of the fire. Jack heard him snoring–a noise that sounded like one hundred foghorns all sounding at once. Jack decided to wait until daylight to make his move, and then, seeing that the giant was still sleeping, he made a grab for the hen, and quietly found his way out of the mansion. Outside, he ran as fast as he could to the beanstalk, and then quickly descended the giant tree, carrying the hen with him.

His mother was overjoyed to see him return. Jack promised that he wouldn't disobey her again, and said that the hen would provide for all the riches that they needed. Sure enough, within very little time, they were very comfortably off.

Jack remained faithful to his mother for a while, but presently remembered the fairy's advice–that he should take as many of the riches from the giant's house as he could, and should never forget that it was his duty to avenge his father's death.

Jack told his mother of his adventure in the land of the giant, and begged her to allow him to make another ascent of the beanstalk. Each time he pleaded with her, his mother became terrified that she would lose him.

"My son, if you go, I fear that I will never see you again. The giant's wife is sure to recognise you a second time, and there are too many dangers that you would need to overcome."

Jack's mind would not be changed, although he felt very guilty for again disobeying his mother. Before making his second journey up the great tree, Jack heavily disguised himself, hoping that by so doing he would not be recognised by the giant's wife as the boy who had come before.

Jack rose early to begin his climb. Reaching the top of the dependable plant, he again found himself in the strange dream world that was the giant's domain. Feeling tired after his climb, Jack made quickly for the giant's mansion.

The giant's wife was standing by the door, as before. To Jack's great relief, she did not recognise him through his disguise.

"Who is this that comes to our door?" she asked.

"I am a poor traveller, looking for a place where I might rest my head, and—if my lady would be so kind—be offered something that I might eat," replied Jack.

"You cannot come in here!" the woman responded sharply, "For my husband is very fond of eating the flesh of people, and he is all the more keen to take young men for his supper, since one who visited here before stole his precious hen from him."

Jack realised that the woman was speaking directly about him. He saw that she believed that he had repaid the kindness that she had shown him by stealing from her husband. The woman implored Jack to find another place where he might stay for the night, but Jack persisted with his request.

Eventually, the woman agreed to allow Jack to stay. He was led through the grand rooms once more, and then along the long gallery, where he could again hear the crying men who were languishing in the dungeon

The giant's wife prepared a supper for Jack and gave him water. Jack could see that she had been badly beaten by her husband, and he feared that she might have suffered on his behalf.

When he had finished his supper, Jack again heard the thunderous steps of the giant, who was approaching the house. Even before the giant came into the kitchen, Jack heard him booming, "Fi, Fi, Fo, Fum. I smell the blood of an Englishman!"

The giant's wife hurriedly ushered Jack into the lumber cupboard, through the keyhole of which Jack could see the giant scolding his wife.

"My husband, I swear, perhaps you can sense the smell of meat brought by some crows to our roof. There is no new human blood here!"

The giant called her a liar, and hit out at her. But she managed to avoid his strike, and calmed him by promising him a fine supper. Presently, he was eating and drinking, seemingly content.

After he had eaten, the giant demanded that his wife bring him something with which he could entertain himself. "Bring me my harp or my money!" he roared.

The poor woman disappeared from the kitchen for a while, returning with two very large bags of coins. The bags were so heavy, that she could only drag them very slowly behind her. The giant seized the first of the bags, and proceeded to count his money.

Jack saw him laying out row after row of silver coins, checking and rechecking that nothing had been taken from his hoard.

When he had finished counting the silver coins, he placed them back in the bag from which they had come, and took up the second bag, which looked as though it was even heavier than the first. This bag contained only gold coins, and as before, the giant took much pleasure laying out and counting his riches, before returning the coins to the bag from which they had come.

His wife left him alone to amuse himself with his money, and when he was finished with his task, he fell asleep in his chair by the fireside. The giant was quickly snoring with the echo of one hundred foghorns, as he had when Jack visited the mansion before.

Jack waited for a while before creeping out of the cupboard, determined to gather up both of the bags if he could. But as Jack reached out for the first of the bags, a small dog that he hadn't noticed before suddenly appeared from beneath the table, barking loudly.

Jack was terrified, certain that the dog would rouse his master. But the giant still slept soundly. Jack managed to find a piece of meat, which he threw across the room to distract the dog's attention. He was then able to lay both his hands on the bags, and make for the main door of the house. He couldn't run, because the bags were so heavy, but eventually reached the top of the beanstalk, there making as rapid a descent as he could, until he arrived back in front of his cottage.

When he came to the cottage, he couldn't see his mother anywhere. The whole house was silent. A little later, a passerby told him that his mother was very sick, and was resting with a kindly neighbour, who lived some miles away.

Jack rushed to see his mother, knowing that he had been unfaithful to his word, and that her sickness may have been caused by his going away.

"My dear mother, I am so sorry that I left you," Jack said when he came to his mother's bedside. "I have been to the giant's house one more time, and have brought for us riches that will allow us to live lives of luxury for the rest of our days."

His mother rebuked him for his disobedience, but seeing that he was safe gave her much pleasure, and within just a few days she was rid of her fever.

"Promise me, my son, that you will never make that hazardous journey again," she insisted.

Jack assured his mother that he would stay by her side, which promise he kept for a period of three whole years. But memory of the fairy's words often returned to him, and he felt certain that he must return one more time to the giant's grand home.

Jack tried to resist the urge to again mount the beanstalk, but his need was too strong. So, he set about making secret preparations for a further visit to the land in the clouds.

Disguising himself once more, lest the giant's wife recognise him as the boy who had visited her before, Jack set about his long climb to the top of the tree. After resting to catch his breath when he completed his ascent, Jack made quickly for the giant's house.

The giant's wife was standing by the door, as Jack expected. She did not recognise him, but repeated her warning that he should stay away from the house. As before, Jack pleaded with her to be allowed to stay for one night, and despite her complaints about the ungratefulness of a young man who had earlier repaid her hospitality by taking her husband's money, the woman led Jack into the house once more.

Through the grand rooms, along the corridor from which the screams of the poor prisoners could be heard, and into the kitchen they went once more. Here, Jack was offered a hearty supper, before the giant's approach was sounded by his deafening footsteps, that became louder as he neared the door.

"Quick, you must hide!" whispered the woman. "Crouch here, inside this large copper."

Jack did as he was told. Fearing that the giant was very close, Jack trembled inside the giant pot. "Fi, Fi, Fo, Fum. I smell the blood of an Englishman!" bellowed the giant.

"No, my husband. No!" cried the woman. "There is nothing new here that you can smell!"

The giant lashed out at his wife, narrowly missing her cheek. "Liar!" he hollered. "Where is the scoundrel hiding?"

Not believing his wife's story, the giant proceeded to search around the kitchen, hunting for the person that he felt sure was close by. He pulled open cupboard doors, and stared angrily into the oven. He peered behind the curtain, and crawled on his knees to see what might be lurking underneath the table. When he began to lift the lid of the copper in which Jack was hiding,

Jack froze solid with fear, but the giant did not lift the lid, slamming it back in its place, as he continued storming around the room.

The giant's wife served her husband's supper, filling his jug with extra wine in a hope that this might calm his temper. Presently, the giant quietened down, and then demanded that his harp be brought to him, so that he might content himself with its beautiful sound.

His wife quickly obeyed, resting the harp in front of the giant. Banging his fist on the table, he thundered his wish for it to "Play!" The magical instrument began playing itself as soon as the order had been given.

Jack was astonished by what he heard, now feeling more confident that he might yet outwit the giant.

When he had finished listening to the harp, the giant fell asleep. Hearing the deafening snoring, Jack gently lifted the lid of the copper to see if it might be safe for him to make his escape. He crept out of the vessel, and made to steal away with the harp.

However, to Jack's great terror, the harp was enchanted with a fairy, who was charged with protecting it. "Master! Master!" came her voice the moment Jack tried to rest his hands on the remarkable instrument.

The fairy's calling awoke the giant. Seeing Jack in front of him, the giant struggled out of his chair and let out a furious roar. "Boy! Boy!" he screamed, "I'm going to tear you limb from limb, and make a meal of your body!"

Jack was terrified, and started to run as fast as he could out of the mansion, then back along the long road toward the beanstalk. Because he could not balance himself well after making himself merry with wine, the giant could only walk slowly, often needing to correct himself to avoid tumbling over. But even a single stride made by the giant counted for many that Jack had to run.

As he raced for the beanstalk, Jack knew that at times the giant was very nearly upon him. But Jack arrived at the giant plant first, and tore down its great ladder more quickly than he had ever done before.

On his way down, Jack cried out to his mother below to quickly bring a hatchet, such that he might cut down the stalk as soon as he made landfall in the garden. His mother quickly found a hatchet, which Jack seized from her as he stepped away from the giant stalk. With a single, mighty blow, Jack drove the hatchet right through the beanstalk, which came tumbling down from the sky.

At the very moment that Jack aimed his blow, the giant had just begun to fumble his way down the ladder. Falling the full height from the clouds to the ground, the giant was felled along with the great tree.

Jack's mother was beside herself with joy to see that her son was safe, and was elated to know that Jack could no longer steal away to climb the beanstalk.

The fairy that had spoken to Jack when he first journeyed to the giant's land then appeared in the garden. She explained to Jack's mother why her son had had to disobey her–that he had needed to avenge the death of his father, whose sad story had been told to him.

Turning to Jack, the fairy exhorted him to be faithful to his mother from that moment on, and to follow the fine example that had been set by his father.

Jack begged for his mother's forgiveness, and promised that he would never more break his promise to her.

Diamonds and durva

People say that we live in a slum, but for my mother and I, ours is the best home in the world. Our house is built from sheets of plywood and corrugated iron, strong enough to survive when the monsoon arrives. I have always lived here through my full thirteen years– in Dharavi, in the city of Mumbai. This is my village, large and brimming with many people though it may be.

I grew up within sight of the Mahim Creek, the large stream of water that borders the village, but my family only came to the city a short while before I was born. Mummy often talks about the village in upstate Maharashtra that was her earlier home, but she always shies away whenever I've asked her to tell me about my daddy, who I never knew.

Mummy has been good to me these past thirteen years. She works at a tannery on the edge of the village, sewing leather hides. With the small wages that she earns, she buys our rice, and, once in awhile, special treats for me. Since our family is small, there are not many mouths to feed, unlike in most of the houses in our neighbourhood.

Mummy makes my clothes, and sings me songs that her mother taught her. Every morning before school begins, we go to the Shree Siddhivinayak Ganapati Temple to offer our prayers to Lord Ganesh. Mummy then makes her way to the tannery, and I join my school friends to begin our day's lessons.

Now that her parents are unable to work, mummy tries to save some of her earnings to send to them when she can. She has already sold most of the few possessions that we have. One day, she asked me to take a treasured jug that she and my father had been given as a part of their dowry. She said that the jug was made of silver, and that a pawnbroker near the Crawford Market should offer a generous price for such a precious item. I promised to find a broker who would pay us the most, and set off on my journey into the centre of the city.

I knew that it was hard for my mother to give up this item, as it had been a gift from her parents. She used it to pour milk from it when I was younger, and so

I too was saddened to see this beautiful memento of my childhood go.

I made my way downtown, pushing through the crowds at Dharavi station to position myself near the edge of the platform for when the train came. The trains were always full by the time they arrived at our station, so it was necessary to act quickly to find yourself a place to stand.

When the train arrived, I grabbed onto one of the large grip handles that hang by the sides of each carriage's entrance ways, then found myself a small foothold on which to secure myself against the side of the train.

I made haste through the crowds when we arrived at the Churchgate terminus, keeping a firm hold on the silver jug, which might prove a profitable steal for an astute thief.

Finding my way to the place that mummy had told me, I waited for my turn to present my ware to the pawnbroker. I carefully handed the jug to a tall man wearing a tiny eyeglass, who proceeded to check its markings and condition from behind his small, splintered counter.

"I will give you 300 Rupees!" he snapped, with a smile. "300 Rupees a good price, don't you think?"

The man seemed to be keen to make the purchase, and I reasoned that 300 Rupees was a fair exchange for my offering, and so I nodded my agreement and handed over the jug.

The man seemed very pleased to have made the deal without further debate, and quickly paid over the money that he'd promised to me.

"Wait! Wait a moment!" he insisted, before disappearing into the back of his small shop. Returning, he brought with him a small packet of what looked to me to be like blades of grass, offering the tiny envelope for me to take.

"Special gift for you!" he said, still smiling. "Durva plant. Brings good luck! Special present for you today!"

Not sure what I had just taken from him, I thanked the man and made my way back through the market, feeling content with the business that I had transacted. I felt certain that mummy would be pleased too.

I could not have been more wrong. When I returned home and excitedly showed my mother the three hundred Rupee notes that I'd brought her, she became very angry.

"300 Rupees! 300 Rupees! Is that all you could earn for our precious family treasure?" she screamed.

Mummy had never screamed at me like this before, while I had felt the back of her hand from time to time, of course.

"300 Rupees is barely enough to buy rice for a week!" she hollered, before collapsing into her chair and starting to cry. I knelt down beside her, curled my arm around her, and offered what I thought would be reassuring words.

"It's not just 300 Rupees that I have brought us, dear mummy," I assured her. "But look, this special plant as well." I took the packet of grass from my pocket, and handed it to my mother. "This is special grass. It brings us luck!"

My new offering didn't stop my mother from crying. Instead, she hurled the packet of grass across the room and screamed even louder. "You stupid boy!" she cried. "What use to us is a packet of grass?"

I did my best to console my mother, but she wanted to be left alone. So I collected the blades of grass that had spilled on the floor, and crept out of the house, making for the temple.

I did not know why mummy was so disappointed with what I had brought. 300 Rupees was a lot of money for me, but it seemed that she had expected more.

At the temple, I left my shoes by the door, and quietly made my way through the crowds, to take my turn to make my devotion to the great Lord Ganesh. When it was time for me to prostrate myself before his beautiful effigy, I first presented my handful of grass to him, as an offering to add to the marigold garlands, sweet-smelling cakes, and fine fruits that had already been paced on his altar.

Kneeling before my great God, I brought my hands together, breathed in the luscious smell of fine incense that filled the temple, and fixed my eyes upon the patient elephant face that stared down at me.

"Dear Lord Ganesha," I prayed. "Mummy thinks that I have been foolish, but I didn't want to bring her sorrow. Please let her forgive me, and show me how I might make for her a better son."

I pleaded with the Lord with all of my heart, and seeing the great kindness in his eyes, felt certain that he had heard my prayer.

After a time, I made as to leave from the temple, bowing before the great Remover of Obstacles one more time, before turning to face the cacophony of car horns, arguing tradesmen, and frantic chatter of the masses that were waiting for me outside.

The temple was my sanctuary, second only to my home as my favourite place. There, I could escape the wild heartthrob of the city for a short while.

Heading away from the temple, my eye was caught by the reflection of a ray of sunlight, bouncing off some dark object that was lying in the gutter. I bent down to see what this might be, and I soon discovered that it was a lady's handbag–and a quite luxurious one at that. I looked inside, and saw that the bag contained a purse that was filled with thousand Rupee notes. For a brief moment, I wondered what I might do were I to hold

onto my find, but it was obvious that I must straight-
away take this to the nearest police station.

I waited my turn to see the clerk at the reception
desk, handed over the bag, and filled out a form to
leave my name and address, in case the officer in
charge of recovered property had any further need to
speak with me.

I made my way home, and related my adventure to
my mother. She had stopped crying, and seemed
pleased that I had passed the bag to the police. "Come
my son," she said, putting her arm around me. "You're
not always such a bad boy! Let me make you supper."

I think that my mother was still angry that I'd not
earned more money for her precious jug, but she never
said any more about this. She loved me dearly, and I
was determined to be a good son for her.

During the next few days, life carried on as though
nothing unusual had happened. However, the following
weekend, we were paid a visit that at first caused my
mother great anxiety.

An officer from the Mumbai Police came to our
house, wanting to speak to me. I felt sure that mummy
thought that I'd gotten myself into some trouble. To
her great relief, the police officer quickly explained
that the lady whose bag I had found wished to offer me
a reward, and had asked if she might meet me. I gratefully accepted her proposal to meet at the Bandra Police Station the following Saturday.

The lady that I met was very elegantly dressed and adorned with expensive jewellery. I felt sure that she must have come from a very wealthy neighbourhood. She at once called me by my first name, rather than addressing me as "boy", as might be normal to make clear my low ranking.

"Rajeev," she began, "I am deeply indebted to you for returning my possession. You were very honest to honour me with this favour. When I checked my bag, I could see that nothing had been taken. I want you to have a small gift as a gesture of my appreciation."

At this point, she reached into her bag–the same one that I had found lying in the gutter–and took out a small black box. "Here, please take this," she insisted. I nervously offered my hands to accept the gift.

"You may open the box now, if you wish," the lady continued. I did as she suggested, and couldn't believe my eyes when I saw what was contained within–a beautiful, gleaming diamond, resting on a small square of black velvet. I had never held anything as valuable as this before.

The woman smiled. "It's nothing," she said, quite casually. "My husband owns a diamond cutting and polishing company. We trade thousands of these every day on the Bharat Bourse."

I was in such a state of shock, that I couldn't find any words that might express my gratitude. But I think that the woman knew that I was almost ready to cry with delight.

She looked at me for a while, simply smiling and enjoying my reaction. Something in her eyes seemed to suggest that she had known me before, but this could not have been, since I never ventured to the richer parts of the city.

"Would you like to come to see where we polish the diamonds?" she asked me after a while.

"My lady, that would be a great honour!" I mumbled in reply.

Just a few minutes later, I found myself sitting beside her in the back of a leather-upholstered white limousine. As the oversized Lincoln Continental glided its way across the city, I looked out through the dark windows of this amazing machine, watching the mad frenzy of people who were rushing around, cutting deals, and gossiping over juice grinding machines. I could barely hear the jangle of noise outside, as the car was well insulated from exterior sound.

"Is the temperature too cold?" the lady asked, aware that I was unfamiliar with such sophisticated air conditioning. "It's very wonderful, lady!" I replied, overawed by the experience of being transported in this way.

After a while, we arrived at a large building in the district of Bandra, not far from the Mithi River. Her chauffeur released the limousine's doors, and bowed to us as we stepped out onto the street.

My tour of the building lasted well over an hour. As we went from room to room, it seemed as though the workers who were cutting or polishing the fine stones worked extra hard when the lady came nearby. No one spoke, and few looked up to catch our eyes.

In one of the rooms, I couldn't help but notice a beautiful girl, who was perhaps just a little older than myself. She looked at me shyly for a brief moment, while continuing on with her work. Just the brief sight of her kind eyes was enough to send my heart racing, but this was not a place for making conversation, nor for interrupting the tour that my generous hostess was leading.

When we had completed out tour, I was taken to a private room, in which a table had been set out ready for a meal.

"Something to eat?" asked the lady, and presently a series of delectable dishes were laid before us.

When our meal was over, I suddenly heard the yelling of a man, whose shouts seemed to be approaching the room where we were sitting. As far as I could tell, he was barking orders at people, complaining about their laziness and uselessness, or some other grave failing that he perceived.

"Quick, you must leave! You must hide!" urged my hostess. "My husband is returning, and he doesn't like me bringing visitors here without his permission."

Quickly, I scurried underneath the table, settling in my hiding place just as the man entered the room.

"You've been up to something!" The man screamed. "Who has been with you, eating in my place?"

"Just a client, my dear husband" the woman replied. "He left just before you returned. I'd arranged for him to be entertained here."

The man didn't give up with his challenging and goading, but his wife seemed well accustomed to dealing with her husband's angry outbursts.

After a while, the couple left the room, and I soon followed after them, carefully searching for an exit to the building.

While I had waited under the table, I had frozen in fear of being discovered. Now, I moved quickly but guardedly, before eventually finding my way back onto the street. Once free from the building, I ran as quickly as I could, back to the safety of my village.

I reflected for a long time on my day's adventure. I had been given a precious jewel, the likes of which I had never seen before. I had been chauffeured in a luxury car, through whose windows I had observed the life on the streets that I felt sure was destined to be mine. I had been taken into a secret world, and seen that even the wives of wealthy men aren't always free from intimidation and suffering.

I related my full story to mummy. She was as astounded by the lady's remarkable gift as I had been, but implored me to promise her that I would not go close by the factory again.

I promised my mother that I wouldn't put myself in further danger, and said that I would take the diamond to market, and use some of the money that I earned from selling it to buy back the silver milk jug that I had given up for a pittance.

The money that I was offered for the diamond, even after paying for the return of our jug, meant that we didn't need to worry about selling anything more to provide for ourselves for years to come, as well as guaranteeing a small income for my grandparents.

Several weeks passed before my mind started contemplating the possibility of visiting the factory once more. I hadn't forgotten the sweet face of the girl that I'd seen in one of the diamond polishing rooms. Night after night, once I'd heard the last of the trains rattling its way over the viaduct that crossed the creek, I would lie awake, just thinking of that brief moment when her eyes caught mine.

One night, when the moon was at its highest, a snake crawled into our house, as they sometimes did. From the corner of my eye, I could see that it was a cobra. I stayed still in my bed, confident that the impressive reptile had no intention of harming us. The snake slowly lunged its body forward, staying close to the outer wall, and then, in an instant, disappeared through a small gap at the foot of the far side of the house.

I was excited and entranced by this spectacle. The memory of the girl in the factory returned to my mind, and I heard a firm voice inside of me, clearly sounding the words, "Kundalini rising. Kundalini rising." This was the first of many nights when this chant was repeated to me.

I made many visits to the temple, asking the Lord Ganesh to perform a miracle for me. I wanted so much to be able to see that girl again—even to speak to her, if that were ever possible.

The brightly coloured statue of the Lord always smiled back at me, but the mighty *murti* never uttered a word.

One day, as I was making my way home after visiting the temple, a large white car drew up beside me. One of the passenger windows gently whirred open, and out peered the familiar face of the lady that I had met before. Taking off her dark, gold-rimmed glasses, she smiled and asked, "Remember me?"

I replied that I would never forget her, nor her kindness to me. She asked whether I might wish to visit the factory again, so that we might again have lunch together. I quickly accepted her invitation, and within a moment, found myself once more enjoying the opulent comfort of her limousine.

When we arrived at the factory, the lady led me straight to the private room where we had taken lunch before. She gave instructions for food to be brought to us, and once more, I was treated to a mouth-watering feast.

Over lunch, my hostess asked me questions about my family. She seemed to be especially interested to learn about my father. I told her that I knew very little about him, because he had died when I was very young.

Throughout our conversation, I longed desperately to ask that I might be allowed to see the polishing rooms once more, where I hoped that I might have a chance to exchange a glance with the beautiful girl that I had seen before. Eventually, feeling emboldened by my desire, I presented my wish to the lady, not shrinking from telling her the true reason for my request.

My kind hostess listened carefully, and smiled as she offered her response. "Of course, Rajeev. It would be my pleasure to show you around once more!"

When we came into the room where the girl was working, my eyes instantly caught upon hers, before she returned to concentrating on the fine work that she was engaged in. No sooner had we made this brief exchange, than I again heard the furious shouting of the factory owner, becoming louder as he seemed to be coming toward us.

"Quick, Rajeev, you must hide!" whispered his concerned wife. I quickly crawled underneath the large worktable at the centre of the room, around which perhaps sixteen or more girls were busy working at their craft. I crept toward what I thought was the seat occupied by the girl whose darling face gave me no sleep at night.

The bullying husband seemed certain that something was being hidden from him, but being a skilled diplomat, my hostess was able to calm him to some extent. Instead, the despot started to take out his anger on some of the workers who were sitting around the table, shouting and swearing, and even lashing out at one or two whose work he considered not to be of sufficient standard.

Trembling, I kept as quiet as I could, fearing that were I to let out as much as sneeze, I would be soon discovered. My heart ached for the girl whose feet I was now crouched beside, desperately fearing that she too might be among those that the ogre lashed out at.

Fortunately, the shouting and scolding soon abated, as the lady who had bought me here led her husband away to another part of the building.

I slowly crept out from underneath the table, pushing myself up into a kneeling position in the small space next to the girl that I had been longing to meet. I realised that this was not a normal way for making an introduction, but my appearance from under the table was not by my design.

"Hello, my name is Rajeev," I began, offering my hand for her to shake. The poor girl looked up from her work, unsure whether she should say anything, and terrified that she might be scolded if she were to be found out for letting her concentration on her task slip even for an instant.

I could see that she was very shy, but she looked very sweetly at me. After a time, she eventually spoke, although very quietly. "My name is Joshika," she said. "You must go quickly before the master comes back!"

I pleaded with her to let me stay a while, and found myself asking, almost quite unexpectedly, whether she might want to meet me for a mango milkshake sometime. The girl stared at me hesitantly, but seeing that I was insistent, eventually agreed to meet me at *The Bagel Shop* in Bandra the following Sunday.

Overjoyed, I waved excitedly at her, almost falling over the trolley of a passing chai waller as I backed my way out of the workshop. Then I set about retracing my steps back to the entrance to the building, before quickly running home. I was uplifted by my latest adventure, but confused by the strange mix of emotions that I felt.

Sunday seemed to take forever to arrive, but eventually the moment came for me to put one of the many possible conversations that had been running through my mind to the test.

To my wonderful surprise, Joshika was already waiting for me at the bagel bar. I ordered two mango shakes from the waitress, and set about finding out as much as I could about this most precious of young women.

Joshika told me that she had been sold by her father to the factory owner at a young age, even before she had been taught to read and write. She worked for sixteen hours most days, and was only allowed one afternoon free each week to enjoy for herself. Her home was a hostel, which adjoined the factory. Twenty girls slept together in a single dormitory, each receiving a bowl of rice twice each day, in addition to the one hundred Rupees that they were paid each month. This was the only life that she had known, and she could see no possibility for her escaping her misery.

My heart burned as I listen to Joshika's sad story—so different to my own—but she was eager to hear my story too.

I told her about the village that my family had come from, of the loss of my father while I was still young, and then related the strange story of how I had come to be a guest of the First Lady of the factory.

"Piloda?" Joshika exclaimed. "I think that's the very village that was once home to a workshop manager who my colleagues often speak about. There was a man called Mr. Doshi, who was well liked by his staff. He worked hard, and always took time to look after the concerns of everyone in his charge."

Joshika paused for a moment, recollecting the details of the story that she'd often been told. "This good man was murdered by Mr. Sahni, the factory's owner," she continued. "At least, that's what the older women in the workshop claim."

Joshika appeared agitated, unsure about whether it was right for her to continue telling her tale. "He was beaten and bruised by Mr. Sahni," she went on. "I'm not sure what he was meant to have done wrong, but he could never have deserved to be pushed against a lathe machine that we use for cutting the diamonds.

"Some of Mr. Sahni's men took the body away, and we never heard any more about what happened. Mrs. Sahni was in the workshop at the time, but she seemed helpless to stop her husband from his monstrous actions."

Joshika ended her story with a grave warning. "Mr. Sahni threatened to kill anyone who ever mentioned what they'd seen or heard".

I promised to keep the story secret, but felt strangely troubled about the identity of the man who had died. If the details of what Joshika had been told were true, this incident would have happened around the time that I believe my father died, and this was a man who had come from the very same village where he had been born.

After our conversation, I walked with Joshika back to her hostel, where we agreed to meet again the following Sunday. However, this time, I didn't need to wait a full week before visiting the factory again.

Early the following week, Mrs. Sahni sent one of her menservants to fetch me–arranging for her smart white limousine to collect me from close by my home, to journey to the factory once more. I was beginning to become quite accustomed to this way of travelling around town, which made for quite a change from my usual habit of clinging to the side of a train.

In the room where I was again offered lunch, Mrs. Sahni explained that she'd asked to speak to Joshika. "Something told me that I needed to find out what she'd been telling you," Mrs. Sahni continued. "Fear not, she has done nothing wrong, and I will ensure that what she has told me will not bring any bad consequence for her."

I was reassured to know that Mrs. Sahni would treat Joshika well. She went on to say that Joshika had related to her what she had told me in the bagel shop.

"This is a story that's known to many in the company," Mrs. Sahni continued. "My husband arranged for the body of the dead man to be dumped off Back Bay, and swore vengeance on anyone who betrayed what had happened to the police–including myself. We've all lived in fear of our lives ever since."

"What was the name of the man who was killed?" I asked. "Maniram Doshi," Mrs. Sahni replied. "By all accounts, he was a good man, always looking after the interests of other people."

I let out a deep sigh and buried my head in my hands. "That was my father!" I cried, struggling to avoid Mrs. Sahni seeing the tears that were beginning to form in my eyes.

She came to put her arms around me, struggling to know what to say, but eventually breaking the silence. "I thought that it might be," she began, "Ever since Joshika told me that your father came from Piloda. You look very much like him, and you clearly are someone of great integrity–just like your father."

I wanted to know why no one had reported Mrs. Sahni's evil husband to the police. It soon became clear to me that she'd wanted to, but had never believed that her husband would be put on trial.

"No one would ever have believed the story," she explained. "My husband covers his tracks well. If the case had ever gone to court, there would have been little evidence that the prosecution could have presented. Your father's body was deposited at sea, and the blood was quickly wiped from the lathe. Accidents with those machines happen all the time, and my husband could easily argue that any blood that might have stayed on the blade was just another example of such an incident."

"Was my mother told?" I asked.

"Yes, but not the full detail. She believes that your father died from an accident at the factory, and that he had to be quickly cremated before she could be found. I understand that she was nursing you at your grandparents' home at the time."

So many questions were turning in my head, but uppermost in my mind was a desire to avenge my father's death.

"Can we not now go to the police?" I asked in desperation. "Surely they would believe your story, and the testimony of all those who witnessed what happened in the factory?"

"My husband is well regarded by many powerful people in this city," she replied dolefully. "Besides which, we have no new evidence to offer."

Mrs. Sahni repeated the threat that her husband had made to her, as well as to others who might consider betraying him. "I would need to flee this place were I ever to go against my husband," she continued.

"You could stay with us," I offered, "No one would ever find you there!"

Mrs. Sahni smiled, and gave me a gentle squeeze.

I could see that the woman who embraced me was no less a slave to her master than Joshika and all the others who laboured for him.

We sat in silence for a while, before the regular hum of the factory was interrupted by the sound of Mr. Sahni making his way toward the lunch room.

Still in a state of shock, I had no time to find a safe hiding place before the door of the room was thrown open. "Caught you at last!" the tyrant hollered at his wife, demanding to know which "client" she was entertaining this time.

Mr. Sahni ran swiftly around the table, then reached his arm back, ready to direct a blow at his wife. But Mrs. Sahni was too quick for her husband, and both she and I managed to escape his grasp, then raced along the corridors of the large building, down several flights of stairs, and through the main entrance.

"Quick, we'll take the Porsche!" Mrs. Sahni yelled, pointing to a gleaming black sports car that was parked just outside. She jumped into the driver's seat, and I quickly took my place by her side.

Mr. Sahni followed close behind us, but hadn't been quick enough to grab at one of the doors of the Porsche before his wife slammed on the central locking. Quickly jumping into the limousine that had been waiting to take me home close by, we knew that the titan had ordered his chauffeur to not lose sight of our tail.

Mrs. Sahni told me that she often liked to drive the Porsche herself, but preferred being outside of the city, where she could put the car through its paces. The weekend of Ganesh Chaturthi, the end of the annual festival celebrated in honour of the Lord Ganesha, was not the best time for demonstrating her motor racing skills in the heart of Mumbai.

Despite its less generous manoeuvrability and broad girth, the limousine loomed large in the Porsche's rear-view mirror.

"I need you to tell me where to go," Mrs. Sahni instructed me, desperately keeping her attention on the road. "I don't know these streets quite as well as I used to."

We managed to lose the limousine on several occasions, but no sooner had Mrs. Sahni put the Porsche into fifth gear, than we ran across a new obstacle ahead of us. Sometimes, it was nearly a pedestrian that we ran into, often one who was ambling too slowly in the middle of the road; at others, it was a cow aiming a disgruntled stare in our direction that caused us to lose distance.

The biggest problem of all was the festival parades that we kept running into. Crowds of people were gathering all over the city to display their beautifully painted clay impressions of Ganesha, which very soon they would take to the beach to send on their way out to sea. The immersing of the Ganapati was always the climax to the thrilling festival.

Whenever we met a new parade, we could do nothing but follow slowly in procession–sometimes finding our windscreen scattered with colour-dyed flour, which some people enjoyed sprinkling around.

When we found ourselves on a clear road, we could quickly gain distance on the Lincoln. Mrs. Sahni showed no fear when dodging between pick-up trucks and donkey traps, as we made for the sweep of the Western Express Highway, the great thoroughfare that hugged the northern coast of Mahim bay.

My plan was to try to lose the Lincoln in the labyrinth of passageways in Dharavi, which I knew so well. But while I knew that the limousine would never be able to navigate the narrow dust tracks of my village, I wasn't sure that the Porsche would be able to either.

Approaching the village, we stayed close to the creek. The Lincoln had gained ground on us, but was having a more difficult task of dodging the many road users that impeded our passage. If we didn't have to dodge to avoid flattening a chicken, in the next instant, we would come face-to-face with a rickshaw that had pulled out from nowhere.

Mrs. Sahni constantly hammered the Porsche's horn to warn would-be trespassers to get out of our way. But this was of little use, because everyone in our city drives with their hands never far from the horn.

We sped toward a small spit of land that wasn't far from my home. A narrow pathway separated a ramshackle of houses from a small causeway that led out into the creek.

"Quick, turn immediately to the left!" I screamed to my driver, unsure whether the Porsche would be able to clear the small street. The passenger side of the car didn't fully clear the street, but the powerful wheels of the Porsche made small-fry of the muddy bank to my left, which capped the upper wall of the causeway.

"Quick! We need to get out here!" I shouted, after we had come to the creekside. "We can run to my house from here. They'll never be able to reach us in that thing!"

As we were unfastening our seat belts and about to leave the car, the Lincoln swerved sharply into the short street that we'd just pulled into. But the narrow track was no match for the limousine. Rather than cruising along the muddy bank as we'd been able to, the right-side wheels of the giant white beast quickly lost contact with the ground–causing the car to over-turn as it toppled on its other side, before quickly sliding down the muddy causeway and becoming caught by the strong current of the creek.

As we jumped out of the Porsche, we saw the great underbelly of the Lincoln being carried under the railway viaduct. We later learned that Mr. Sahni had opened the window of the limousine in an attempt to escape, but had been drowned by the pungent sewage that flowed into the creek, before he had a chance to break free from the car.

Mrs. Sahni and I returned to the Porsche, then drove to a safe place where we could park, close to mummy's house.

My mother was astonished to see that I had brought such a finely dressed visitor to our home, but was happy to see that I had returned safely, having been out of the house for much longer than she had expected.

"I thought that you would be too late for going to the beach," she said. "Tonight is the night you've waited many months for, the night we send the Ganapati on his way."

"Mummy, allow me to introduce Mrs. Sahni," I interrupted, aware that my mother didn't know how to bring herself to ask how I came to be bringing this high caste lady into our house.

I told my mother the whole story. Mrs. Sahni offered her deep condolences for the loss of my father many years before. She promised that his memory would be honoured with a special plaque at the factory, and said that she wanted my mother and I to feel that we were now a part of her own family.

Mummy prepared a meal of *modak*, which our guest accepted graciously. "You are a very fine cook, Mrs. Doshi," she said. "You cook much better food than anything I ever eat at the factory!"

We joined together to celebrate the end of the festival, singing the familiar *Sukhakarta Dukhaharta*, before making for the beach to watch the clay models of Lord Ganesha being launched into the sea. We cheered and sang as one followed another into the water.

"Will you look after Joshika?" I asked Mrs. Sahni, as we watched fireworks explode over the bay. "Of course I will," she promised. "In fact, I think that I will have another job for her soon—one that will allow her more time to spend with a certain young man!" She smiled, then turned to applaud the fireworks that were making more beautiful the always colourful tableau of life that is Mumbai.

Afterword

Jack and the beanstalk tells the story of a boy achieving manhood. Through various ordeals and discoveries, Jack learns to find his own way in the world, and so moves to both sexual and social maturity.

Jack's mother is at pains to prevent her son from exploring the world himself. Her response to his first act of self responsibility—selling the cow—is to punish him, and she constantly warns him against climbing the beanstalk, pointing to her own worries about losing her son.

Jack's main challenge is to resist his mother's urgency to hold on to him as her baby child. In doing so, he encounters his Oedipal father figure in the giant, who is both his adversary and sparring partner, and through whom he ultimately learns his ability to face manhood.

For Jack, life was sugarcoated before his mother instructed him to sell the cow. When the reliable source of milk is gone–in reality, Jack being weaned from his mother–he must learn to provide for himself and his family.

Jack is at first enticed by a magical world. He eagerly takes the mysterious seeds in exchange for the cow, believing that these will provide a solution for the family's needs. Once the seeds have been planted, it takes no time at all for him to discover a whole new fantasy world.

The land of the giant is where Jack learns that the real world is beset with dangers. To survive, he must rely on his own initiative, knowing when to accept offers of help that are made to him (as in the case of the hospitality and protection provided by the giant's wife).

Despite gaining a valuable treasure to provide for his family after his first visit, Jack cannot help but retreat into the fantasy land for a second and third time, even though he is aware of the great dangers of doing so. It is only after his third visit that he realises that he must overcome his attempts to escape reality, and face up to his responsibilities in the real world.

The prizes that Jack brings home are a hen that can lay golden eggs (a continuing source of food provision), and two bags filled with valuable coins (money to sustain the family's needs). He thus learns that he must provide a continuing means for sustenance, and to do this involves using his wit, physical strength, and resolve.

His stealing away from his mother to climb the beanstalk, and his hiding from the ogre when in the giant's mansion (his Oedipal father), point to Jack's embarrassment of exploring his sexuality in the full glare of his parents. However, he persists with his exploration, and ultimately matures into a man who is able to face his parents on adult terms.

While the phallic significance of the *Beanstalk* story alludes to masculine sexuality, its essential messages are also relevant for girls who are coming to maturity. As with many fairy stories, the gender of the lead character can be readily swapped without losing the meaning of the tale.

The princess and the pea

A young prince desperately wanted to find a princess who he could ask to be his wife. He wanted to be certain that he would marry a real princess. He therefore resolved to travel far and wide to seek out the one that he could be sure was meant to be his true love.

Seeing that their son was sincere in his quest, the old king and queen wished him well as he set off to find his bride.

The prince travelled through many kingdoms, exhausting both himself and his horse. He met many fine young maidens who went by the name of a princess. But the prince was never sure whether any who he met were real princesses. Something never seemed to be quite right, although he couldn't explain to himself why he felt so uncertain.

After many months and many miles of travelling, the prince decided to return home to his own kingdom. "How many beautiful maidens I have met," he mused. "How often have I wondered whether one might be mine? But my heart will not let me choose any from among them."

Deeply saddened, he led his horse home and re-solved to stay close to his parents until his true bride might be found.

One night, there was a ferocious storm that swept across the kingdom. Ancient trees that had seen many centuries come and go were torn from the ground and thrown onto their sides. Terrifying lightening ripped across the sky, turning the darkness of night into a bright bluish light. Thunder roared in all directions, and the rain fell so heavily that soon many of the streets turned to rivers.

The king and his household gathered around the grand fireplace in the banqueting hall, for they could not sleep while the storm raged outside.

Suddenly, there came a knocking on the castle's gate.

"Who might that be at this hour, coming here in such terrible conditions?" asked the king. "I will go with my guards to see who is troubling us."

And so the king went down to the gate and asked who was knocking.

"It is I," came a faint voice from the other side, "A princess from a neighbouring kingdom. Please allow me entrance to your castle, Your Majesty, as I am wet through from the rains and exhausted after my journey."

"Very well," said the king, and he ordered his guards to open the castle's gate.

When the gate was opened, the king saw a pitiful looking creature standing in front of him. Her hair hung in tangles over her shoulders. Her skin shuddered from the cold. Her clothes were so wet through that she could barely stand straight in them.

The king saw that the poor girl could not be left out on her own in the storm.

"Come this way," said the king, beckoning the girl to follow him to the banqueting hall. There he introduced her as being a princess from a neighbouring kingdom, as she had told him.

"But are you a true princess?" asked the prince.

"Oh yes, my Lord. Truly I am!" the princess replied.

The old queen was not convinced by her story. "We'll soon see if you're telling the truth," she said. Without a further word, she then disappeared off to the bedchamber that was being prepared for the girl's stay.

The queen placed a single pea on the bottom of the bedstead on which the girl would sleep, and instructed her servants to pile not just one, but twenty mattresses on top of each other, each with an eiderdown to cover it.

"This will test whether she is a real princess or not!" exclaimed the queen.

The girl was led to the room and left alone for the night. She climbed right to the top of the twenty mattresses and lay down her head to sleep. But try as hard as she might, and after much tossing and turning, she could not get comfortable and could not fall asleep. The bed felt very hard at the point where the pea lay, although she didn't know that the queen had secretly placed anything there.

Soon, the princess was covered in bumps and bruises, and she found herself lying wide-awake, nursing her pain. Her tears spilled onto her pillow as she fought for just a moment's peace.

The following morning, the queen knocked on the girl's chamber door to ask her how well she had slept in the bed of twenty mattresses.

"Oh my queen, I must confess, I had a terrible night! I could not sleep at all! Something under the mattresses was so hard that I could do nothing but toss and turn all night in an effort to get comfortable. As you can see, now I am black and blue all over!"

The queen was astounded. "My dear, truly you are a real princess!" she said. "No one other than a real princess would be so delicate as to feel the pea that had been placed under the twenty mattresses. The king and prince must be told immediately!"

And so, the princess joined the royal household in the banqueting hall, and the prince was overjoyed to hear the news that he had finally met a real princess.

"Dear princess," asked the Prince, "If you will allow me the honour, it will give me the greatest pleasure if you would be happy to be my wife."

"My dear prince," replied the princess, "I have known that my heart was made for yours since I first saw you. Nothing would give me greater pleasure than to share my life with you."

And so the two were married in a splendid ceremony, the likes of which had never been known before. The king and queen welcomed the princess as their own daughter, and the entire kingdom celebrated the joining of two perfect hearts.

As for the pea–well, that was put in a museum for all to marvel at. You might see it still were you to visit.

This is a true story.

Manhattan transfer

I've given up trying to defend my profession. The truth is, I never really cared. Most of us bankers are total wankers, at least ones like me who used to spend our days placing bets with other people's money. We didn't care that the world's economy teetered on collapse. That didn't stop our closed party, nor make a blind bit of difference to the bonuses that we earned.

Now I see how much I hated working in that place. One massive sea of computer screens and arseholes shrieking and swearing at each other. No one ever showed an ounce of interest in anyone else. To get anywhere in the bank, you had to become a prime arsehole, learn how to humiliate and scream at anyone who might do you favour and know how to treat the back office staff like shit.

There was some show of being a company made up of people–drunken nights out at the Bowery, obscene tabs run up at *Bill's West Side Bar*, and the annual sortie to Emerald Bay in the Bahamas, the bank's way of showing its "gratitude" for our latest busting of targets.

This was all just macho bravado. No one there really thought about anyone else, and more and more I found myself turning into one of the monsters that surrounded me. It's true what's said–money doesn't buy happiness.

Travelling first class on business trips became as mundane to me as taking a cab across town. No luxury room or flashy lobby in the many hotels that I stayed in came close to exciting my senses or giving me anything new to appreciate. I came to expect nothing other than perfection, and my beloved colleagues in the trading room taught me the skills to belittle and shame even the most arrogant of idiots that might attempt to stand in my way.

I had a smart apartment on the Upper West Side, overlooking Central Park. Deep-pile Wilton carpets, freshly laundered linen laid out on my bed each morning by the minions that I employed to organize my life, three closet-fulls of designer dresses, snapped up from whichever Fifth Avenue boutique I happened to be passing, not to mention my prized collection of couture shoes.

Not that I usually saw much of my home outside of odd weekends. A trader's life involves selling your soul to the bank. My normal routine was to ride the subway to the office before six each morning, often not returning home until after midnight.

Once sitting at my desk on the 22nd storey, I rarely stopped to remember that there was a world outside. Life went on behind the tinted glass of the faceless building on Murray Street where I spent my days–the vessels plying their trade on the Hudson, and as night fell, a million flickering lights over Manhattan bearing witness to a million or more different stories of anonymous lives.

Being one of only a few chicks on the trading floor, I'd been the prize of a few of my male colleagues' conquests; at least, that's what I let them believe. Their Lamborghini's and skylight jacuzzis did nothing for me, and their sex lived up to their promises only in their imaginations.

I'd learned how to deal with men. I had to. To get where I am in this place, I'd quickly learned to brush off their pathetic patronizing and sexist jibes, and I'd been gifted with the intelligence and turn of phrase to outwit the best of them.

I probably would still have been in that hellhole were it not for 9/11.

I was in Chicago on a business trip at the time. The images that flickered on the TV screen hanging from the wall of the hotel suite near O'Hare where I was meeting seemed unreal, like some crazy dream that had got mixed up with a memory of an action movie seen the day before.

Returning to Manhattan, it became clear to me that the devastating attacks had been all too real. The Twin Towers had stood just a few blocks from my office. I knew a couple of people who worked there, who had miraculously managed to get away before the second tower collapsed.

Suddenly, the circus life of money-making and sucker-screwing that I was leading seemed unimportant. People like me had died, gone forever. Their bodies and faces were so burned and twisted that they were unrecognizable even to their distraught families. I could so easily have been one of them. If those maniacs could bring down the Twin Towers, then nothing could stop them charging another airbus into our place.

After my first day back in the office following my stay in Chicago, I sat like a zombie on the subway carrying me home. As the train made an attempt at speed along its express track, I noticed my reflection in the window opposite–occasionally merging with a streak of white as we raced through a station, or the blurring of anonymous bodies occupying a passing train. The train was jammed, the IRT being one of the few lines still running in the days after the attacks.

I'd been aware of the furrow lines etching ever-deeper ravines into my brow for some time now, and I was only twenty-seven. I'd put this early onset of ageing down to the wear and tear of the job, and placed my trust in the expensive lotion that some pompous twit at Macy's had sold me—a lotion that promised to be the saviour of my skin. But in this moment, I looked a total wreck. I barely recognised the person that I'd become, so far removed from the person that I was when I left High School not even ten years before.

"Why the fuck am I doing this?" I demanded of myself in a rare moment of awareness. "Why do I give my life over to those wankers every day?"

I'd thought about leaving the bank many times, perhaps getting a modest condo out-of-town in Connecticut, perhaps in Greenwich, where I might get myself a boat to mess around with too.

I had the money, of course, but the adrenaline of making a killing drove me back to that hellhole of a place time and again. It's true that I had sold my soul to the bank, but this was one contract that needed to be undone. I came up with the idea of booking myself into a retreat, someplace out in the country where I could get myself together again and work out my next move.

I called in as sick the next morning and quickly hunted down a recovery center near Deville, New Jersey, that specialised in providing sanctuary for burned-out professionals, alongside rehabilitating junkies and alcohol addicts. Not caring whether I might be fired for deserting my post, I packed a small overnight bag and checked in at the retreat the next morning.

"You're lucky we had a room," commented the tender-skinned woman who welcomed me at the reception. "Things have gone crazy here these past couple of days, since the madness started. Smart move to get here right away before they all start banging on our door."

I hadn't clocked that she was right. Sure enough, there'd be thousands upon thousands of traumatized victims soon needing help, not just those who managed to get away and the loved-ones of those who didn't, but all those involved in the rescue operation, and anyone–*anyone*–who lived and worked in the city.

A colleague of the receptionist showed me to my room and left me alone to settle in. I had a first floor room, with tall French doors opening up onto the grounds outside. A freshly mowed lawn gave way to a vista of patchwork fields and isolated farm buildings beyond. A lively play of water sounded its presence as it impacted with the ground surrounding the ornate fountain in the middle of the lawn.

For the first time that I could remember in years, I heard birdsong. But what I liked most about this place was the feeling, a sense of calm that I'd been aware of as soon as I arrived. I knew that the king-sized bed, decorated with its antique lace throw, guaranteed me a welcome place to rest my head.

There was no pressure to take part in any of the activities that were put on at the center each day–mainly various types of therapy, along with relaxation, guided meditations, painting classes and the like. I soon learned that it was foolish to miss out on the three meals that were provided each day, rediscovering the pleasure of home-made dishes–something that I'd rarely known in my other-world existence back home, where I lived off gourmet-prepared home deliveries, or by dining out at some classy downtown restaurant.

Within a day of arriving at the center, I had no doubt that my life had reached a turning point. I phoned into the office the next day to give notice of my resignation, citing my wish to take time out, and needing to restart my life right away if I was able.

As if I needed confirmation of my employer's real appreciation for my five years' of service, they didn't seem too bothered by my suggestion that I use my accumulated vacation time in lieu of serving my notice. "That's up to you," snapped the disinterested HR director when I made my proposal, "Your gate card will be cancelled, and your documents will be ready for you to collect after tomorrow." With barely a further word, she cut short the phone call.

Like most others who'd found their way to the center, I preferred to take the same seat for mealtimes.

It was here, over maple syrup waffles, blueberry muf-
fins and mashed up scrambled eggs, that I first met
Beth.

Beth was nothing like me, albeit we were of a similar age. There was very little that you could say was
cultivated about her. Her straight, pink-punk dyed
hair looked unkempt, her choice of arm tattoos–and
others that I was later to discover–left much to be desired, and her nose-ring detracted from her cute and
finely featured face.

Beth came from Brooklyn, and had been brought to
the center by her parents, in an attempt to help her
finally crack her addiction to gin. I doubt that she
could have afforded to stay there were it not for their
support, as her occasional work selling her Dali-like
paintings could hardly have earned her any more than
a basic living.

Despite our differences, Beth and I formed an immediate bond. We seemed at first to have nothing in
common, apart from our shared need to rid ourselves of
our miserable lives outside. I felt strangely protective
toward her, concerned for her vulnerability, and desperate to see her make a real attempt at kicking her
habit. She was energised by the sudden attention that I
was giving her, enjoyed my tales of high living, and
seemed to want to know everything about what makes
a rich girl like me tick.

Beth and I went for our separate therapies during the day, but we spent many hours chilling out together in the common room, walking down to the fields to see if we could attract any interest from the two mares that grazed on the other side of the fence. We attempted to outdo each other at Scrabble, and made late-night raids on the cookie jar, which was always kept well stocked by the kitchen staff.

Beth was clearly struggling to beat her addiction. Drying out is never easy for anyone, but she had the added worry of not letting her parents down, who, she confided to me, had come to her rescue many times before. She had come back to living at home with them after running away from a complicated relationship. I didn't ask her too much about her past, but I knew that she preferred girls to guys. It's shameful of me to judge, I know, but I'd sussed this pretty much as soon as we met, looking at the way that she dressed and no-ticing what little interest she took in my stories of my sleeping around with the jerks at the office.

Beth's four-week course of treatment came to an end several days before I planned to leave the center. I'd made no plans about my next move, other than to just sleep as much as I could, making up for the many hours that I'd lost when I was giving my all for the bank.

Beth seemed very keen that we should keep in touch after she left, and I felt pleased to have made a new friend–perhaps the one new true friend that I'd made in many years.

Before her parents came to collect her, we exchanged addresses and phone numbers, and she pleaded with me to drop by when I was back in town.

"My parents can be a bit neurotic about who I bring home," she warned me, "But I'm sure that they'll get on just fine with you."

In the privacy of her room, we stood for a brief moment glancing at each other in silence, allowing the unheard voices of our souls to acknowledge the depth of friendship that we'd nurtured during those few brief weeks. Hesitating, Beth cupped her hands around mine, and slowly brought her face toward me, kissing me gently on the lips. "I love you, Levi," she uttered, dropping her embrace and stepping back. "I hope that we'll continue to be friends," she said, before passing me a final glance, taking hold of her rucksack, and slipping out of the room.

I stood for a moment in the space that she'd just vacated. The furious, angry, charcoal sketches that she'd plastered over the walls were gone now. The bed was left made up as best she could. Emptied of her colourful belongings, the empty chest of drawers and half-opened wardrobe had returned from being purveyors of life to their normal, clinical functioning as mere furniture.

I gazed through the window, focusing on the two mares that were grooming each other straight ahead of me, which were seemingly unaware–or at best disinterested–in all that was happening around them.

"I think I might love Beth," I breathed to myself. "Maybe I'm just fond of her, concerned for a troubled friend. But I feel more than a shallow longing within my body. I think that the memory of her gentle kiss will linger with me for more than a fleeting moment."

I'd never tried it on with a girl before, but the more I thought about it, the more determined I became to explore this possibility. Even though I'd only just met her, Beth's face started to loom large in my mind's eye, and I found it easy to see myself being drawn into a full embrace with her, our tongues interlocking with each other, our arms reaching for an ever-firmer grip to squeeze our pulsating bodies together.

I checked up on Beth soon after I was discharged from the center. I took a cab to the address that she'd given me, but waited a minute to take in the atmosphere of the place. I was surprised how few times I'd been to Brooklyn, but that's the nature of most of us New Yorkers. We rarely venture far outside of our own neck of the woods unless we have to. I'd travelled to Europe and Asia several times before, but had never seen any more than VIP airport lounges, limo interiors, hotel suites and soulless offices.

My time in New Jersey had convinced me that I needed to get out of town more, and this prompted an idea to put to Beth.

Making for Beth's house, I mounted the broad flight of steps that led to the double-door of the 1920's brown brick row house. I located the bell button for Beth's parents' apartment, and waited for a reply.

"Hello, who's there?" came a voice, which I assumed to be Beth's mother.

"Hi, my name's Levi, a friend of Beth Dean, and I was wondering if she's in at the moment?" I replied.

"Sure, she's mentioned you many times, and was hoping that you'd pass by soon. We're at the end of the corridor on the fourth floor," she said. I heard the buzz of the door release a couple of seconds later, and I made my way inside.

The place smelt a bit inside, but had a sort of faded grandeur that quite appealed to me. I chose to take the stairs rather than the gated elevator, which looked as though it might struggle to make it to the fourth storey.

The apartment door was already open when I turned onto the landing.

"Welcome honey, it's great to see you!" announced Beth's mom, who was waiting by the door. "Beth will be here in just a moment after she finishes her shower, but let's fix you something to drink."

Beth's mom seemed welcoming. On my first impression, her dad seemed friendly enough too, if a little quiet. We spent a few moments chatting together in their lounge, before Beth came into the room and threw open her arms to greet me. I got up to accept her embrace.

"It's great to see you, Levi!" she cried. "I hope you can hang around for a while," she continued. "I'm sure mom and dad will be happy if you want to stay."

"Well that will be just fine," interrupted Mrs. Dean. "We're always pleased to get to know any new friend of Beth."

I hadn't planned to stay any more than a few hours, and made my excuses–pointing out that I hadn't presumed that I would be invited to stay, and so hadn't arrived with my overnight bag.

Later, when Beth and I were alone, an opportunity arose to put my idea to her. I came straight out with my question, "How d'you fancy going away together for a few days?"

"I was thinking about really getting away, you know, somewhere way out in the sticks, somewhere where we could really be alone for a while. Think it might fly?"

Beth didn't hesitate before responding. "That would be brilliant!" she said, "But I'll need to check first that it's okay with my folks. They can be a bit

funny about me going anywhere, especially with someone I've only just met."

I was surprised by the control that Beth's parents
seemed to hold over their adult daughter, but given her
troubled past, I decided that they must have their rea-
sons, and let the comment go.

Beth put the suggestion to her parents after I'd left.
They agreed to let her go away with me, but her mom
warned her about getting involved too quickly with
such a confident, strong woman that she hardly yet
knew.

I quickly booked a long weekend stay at an old
farmhouse near Smithburg, New Jersey.

Beth had warned me not to bring my Porsche to
pick her up, worried that this might attract unwanted
attention in the street. But we drove through town
without anyone as much as looking at my car, and were
soon cruising over the George Washington Bridge and
heading south on the New Jersey Turnpike.

Our bolthole lived up to its billing on the website
that I'd booked it through. A tidy weatherboard house,
surrounded by various scattered barns and other out-
buildings. It had ceased being used as a farm some
years before, but the house was well cared for by a
nearby villager, who looked after the property while
the landlord was away.

Between us, Beth and I had a choice of five rooms to
bunk down in. She'd already considered my suggestion

that I made on our way down that we share a room and–if she felt comfortable–make use of just one bed.

Given the intensity of feeling that had been growing between us, Beth hadn't hesitated in agreeing with my plan. In fact, I don't think that either of us wanted to do much else. Her parents were now far away, and Beth wasn't quite as incapable of looking after herself, nor as naive as they might sometimes give her credit for.

We settled on the master bedroom, and unpacked our bags.

The house's kitchen was well equipped, leaving me with no excuses for not trying my hand at some basic cooking–my first attempt at throwing together my own meal in many years. Beth didn't seem too bothered by the coarseness of the soup, nor the nauseating taste of the over-fried onions, and we settled together in front of the fire with a couple of mugs of steaming coffee. I felt very settled with Beth's head resting on my shoulder. I just wanted to hold her–she already felt like much more than a good friend.

We teased each other over a couple games of Scrabble, then made our way to bed. Both of us were too tired to do any more than slip under the eiderdown and cuddle up to each other. We both quickly fell asleep, an effort made easier by the fact that there were not one, but three thin mattresses stacked on top of each other on the bed, together with a whole mound of cushions that were piled high to rest our heads upon.

My sweet, peaceful evening and descent into a contented slumber was soon violently interrupted. I was suddenly awoken by the sound of my name being called by a man whose voice I didn't recognise, his words getting ever louder and more distinct. "Levi, Levi, Open your eyes!... Levi, Levi, Open your eyes!"

Beth stirred slightly, but didn't awake. I pushed back on the bed, levering myself into an upright position against the headboard. As my eyes slowly adjusted to the shadowy surrounds, I saw a finely dressed man standing at the end of the bed. He wore classic 1940's-style spectacles and I noticed a badge that was pinned to his apparel, which bore the initials "NSAC". "What on earth does this mean?" I wondered. "But more importantly, who is this standing here?"

I felt certain that I wasn't in a dream. As my eyes gathered more light and my surrounds came more fully into focus, I noticed details that I knew to be real. The floral mug of cocoa that Beth had left half drunk, still sitting on her side table, the three small pictures of coastal scenes hanging on the wall to the right, the large brown trunk carefully squeezed on top of the wardrobe, and the glass wall clock right ahead of me, reliably showing the time as one-fifteen.

"Who the devil are you?" I asked, feeling surprisingly self-assured and not at all afraid.

The man stared at me for a while, and then showed me his right hand. He proceeded to loosen the button fastening his shirt's sleeve and peeled the garment back to reveal what looked like a deep knife wound running across his wrist. I looked directly at his eyes in astonishment, but he didn't say anything, merely glancing at me, as though interested to make my acquaintance. But then, he smiled and adjusted his dress, gave a small bow, and disappeared from my view.

Now fully awake, I began to trouble over who this strange person might be. How did he know my name? Why was it me rather than Beth that he wanted to see? And what about the horrible bloody wound on his wrist–what was his reasoning for showing me that?

I remained calm, but fully alert and preoccupied with what I'd observed. But increasingly, I was troubled by the experience, unable to find any possible answers to the questions that it brought to mind. And so I spent the first night of our vacation staring into the dark space of the room, waiting for dawn to arrive.

I waited until after breakfast to relate my experience to Beth, uneasy that she might think me crazy for feeling the need to share such a wild fantasy. But if this was to be another test of our friendship, I resolved, "so be it".

Beth listened carefully to my testimony, but couldn't offer any fresh thoughts that might explain who it was that I might have seen. "The man who you describe does sound a lot like my grandfather," she offered. "But why would he want to introduce himself to you here, especially since as far as I'm aware, he's lying six foot under in a cemetery out near Flushing Meadows–and why the wound on his wrist?"

It was clear that the mystery of my strange apparition wasn't going to be solved during our brief stay in New Jersey, but both Beth and I were left puzzling over a phone call from her mother that she received later that morning.

We had set off walking in the hills, but were still within cell phone range. "How are you getting on, my dear?" I overheard Beth's mom asking her. "I'm fine, mom. Stop worrying. It's a lovely place and Levi and I are getting on very well."

The pair exchanged trivial conversation for a few moments, and then Mrs. Dean asked Beth if she would pass the phone to me.

"Hello dear, how are you?" she enquired. "Beth says that you're having a great stay out there in the sticks! How did you sleep last night?"

This seemed like an odd question to ask, but I had a strong sense that I needed to answer truthfully.

"To be frank, it was a very strange night, Mrs. Dean," I replied. "This might sound very strange, and I'm not sure why I mentioning this, but I had a sort of vision last night that kept me wide-awake right through until dawn. There was a man standing at the end of my bed, calling my name, and this caused me to wake up from what had been a deep sleep."

"What did the man look like?" Mrs. Dean continued.

"He was about seventy, had wispy grey hair, and wore a pair of black-rimmed spectacles–the traditional 1940's look. Oh, and he wore a lapel badge bearing the initials "NSAC". Strangest of all, he showed me his wrist, which looked as though it had been slashed right through."

"Oh that's lovely, dear," she replied, and then asked that she might again speak with Beth. They continued with their conversation, which, from what I could overhear, sounded as mundane as the way it had started.

I wondered why Beth's mom had seemed to respond so casually to the story that I'd related to her. Did she think that I was a crank, prone to making up wild stories? Or perhaps was she slightly deranged herself? We continued our walk before I broached the matter with Beth.

"Your mom didn't seem to think it at all strange that I had such a bizarre night," I began. "She just said, 'Oh that's lovely, dear', and then asked to be put back to you. Do you think she thinks that I'm a crank?"

"That's just my mom," said Beth. "She's never surprised by things like that. In fact, she's been involved with a spiritualist church in Brooklyn for many years now, part of the National Spiritualist Association of Churches."

"So that's what the letters on the badge must mean!" I interrupted, "NSAC!" I don't know why this came to me so suddenly, but Beth simply replied, "Yes, that's what they call it."

It would be several weeks before we discovered the full truth of what had happened the previous night. I did my best to put the episode out of my mind, wanting to enjoy every moment that I spent together with Beth. Our friendship blossomed, and I rediscovered the joy of cooking and the beauty of nature, something that has passed me by when I worked in that hellhole on Murray Street.

Beth and I met regularly after we returned from our trip, and I did manage to stay over at her folks' home a couple of times in the months that followed. On the most recent of these occasions, her mom finally opened up about what really happened that night on the farm, as we watched *Dancing with the stars* with her in the lounge.

"I have a confession to make," she began. "I invited the man that you saw by your bedside at the farmhouse to pay you a visit. You described him perfectly. It was my father that showed you the cut on his wrist, something even Beth doesn't know about. He took his own life when she was small, but we never told her the real story about how he died. I'm so sorry, dear," she said, turning to Beth, "But we didn't think you could handle it at the time."

Beth bowed her head and started to cry. I put my arm around her, and tried as best I could to let her know that I shared her grief.

Mrs. Dean continued, "I used an old pagan ritual to call upon your grandfather's assistance." Turning back to look at me, she went on, "I asked that he might help me know whether you are meant as a true friend for Beth. He said that he would honour my wish and pay you a visit, but that you would only be able to see him and hear his voice if your heart was in tune with the beat of our baby. When I called Beth the following morning, I was overjoyed to hear that you'd entertained his visit so well! Only someone with the right heart for my daughter would be able to do that!"

Beth and I sat in silence for a few moments, trying to make sense of what we'd just heard. "Why didn't you just allow us to find our own way?" I eventually asked.

"Beth has been badly bruised too many times in the past," she replied. "She seemed so happy with you and I had a good instinct about you, but I wanted to be sure that you are right for her. This was the only way I knew how to find out. I'm sorry that I couldn't tell you before now, but please believe me when I say that I had both of your best interests at heart. I want you to be happy, and I'm so pleased that you seem to be doing so well together."

It took Beth and I some time to come to terms with what we'd heard, but we both knew that Mrs. Dean was sincere in her intention, even if her means for testing us was unconventional. Both of Beth's parents seemed to be genuinely happy that our relationship was growing, and her mom promised that she would never rely on psychic means to interfere with our lives again.

All of this happened some ten years ago now. Beth and I are looking forward to marrying in the summer. Her folks are busying themselves with preparations, promising to make it the best wedding ever.

I gave up my apartment on the Upper West Side. Beth moved in with me when I bought a condo in Stamford, Connecticut. We enjoy walking our dog down by Long Island Sound, and I've become quite the home-carer–baking cakes and concocting new recipes. Beth focuses on selling her artwork. She's been off the bottle since leaving the center where we met in New Jersey. I've never shed a tear for leaving behind the high life that once promised so much.

Afterword

The princess and the pea is the shortest of Hans Christian Andersen's stories, but it has been open to interpretation in many different ways.

The central theme of the story is the quest that both the prince and princess have embarked upon. The prince's quest is explicitly made known to us–to find his true love, the one who will complement him and make him whole. We might assume that the princess had started on a similar mission. While we do not know why she was wandering alone in the middle of a storm, clearly she had been drawn to the castle, and felt compelled to plead for an audience there.

The old king and queen might seem to be bystanders in the story, but both play their part in bringing the prince and princess together. The motherly queen devises a test for the princess and is overjoyed when she succeeds in passing this. Perhaps the queen's joy is not just in the princess being able to open the door to her son's future happiness, but also in finding a daughter-in-law whose qualities are befitting for serving the needs and caring for the well being of the kingdom in her future role as queen[7].

The king in turn takes pity on the drenched young creature that greets him at the castle gate and offers

---

[7] The many princes and princesses who are referred to in fairy stories might be considered as archetypes, rather than elevated members of society. In the story of *The princess and the pea*, the princess shows that she has developed noble values that will later equip her for taking on a responsible maternal role.

her hospitality. As often happens in life, heroines and heroes often step in to help us find our way when we are lost and alone. But we must be ready to open the door, or to respond to a call, when we hear the knocking of someone waiting outside.

The prince does not give in to temptation during his initial flight in search of his life's companion, despite, we might assume, meeting many would-be courters. Instead, he remains faithful to his heart's leading, and is drawn inward in his quest for true love (symbolized by his returning home to his kingdom).

Several Jungian analysts[8] have suggested that the coming together of the princess and the prince represents the joining of the *anima* and *animus*–the feminine and masculine components of the psyche that need to be in balance for an individual to become whole.

Whether or not this is what is intended, the suggestion that both the prince and princess are looking for their true, authentic selves does seem clear. Authenticity is an important theme in the story, and both the prince and princess succeed in proving themselves to be genuine.

Some have suggested that the princess's complaints about her uncomfortable night expose her as some

---

[8] Jungian analysts: Those who study the work of Carl Jung. Jung's work emphasizes the search for wholeness and the "depth psychology" of the unconscious.

kind of diva or precocious child who is never satisfied. Their reasoning is that she becomes obsessed with something as insignificant as a pea, making this the subject of a tantrum, while overlooking the riches that surround her in the form of the twenty mattresses and the hospitality of the royal household.

However, this interpretation seems unlikely given that the princess holds off from saying anything about her condition until she is asked the next morning. She does not complain about being drenched by the rain when brought into the castle either, nor seem to be concerned by what must have been her un-prepossessing appearance. But when she is asked how she passed the night, she doesn't shrink from telling the truth in plain and unambiguous terms.

Image doesn't matter here. We're not told that the princess was beautiful, but only that she is the right person to marry the prince. Indeed, the fact that she arrives at the castle in a bedraggled state highlights the fact that what is meant for us doesn't always appear in quite the way that we might expect–in the case of a princess, perhaps, as a beautiful young woman who is immaculately coiffed and dressed. It takes great sensitivity to see through the outward appearance of a person, to appreciate their true self.

Similarly, the many mattresses that are laid one on top of another represent the multiple layers that need to be stripped away to reveal the core that's buried underneath. Being able to tune in to the heart with full authenticity involves stripping away at the many layers of pretension that conceal our true selves.

Hence, far from being a story about over-sensitivity in women, as many nineteenth-century readers might have interpreted the story, it is an allegory of deep sensing and self-knowing. Sensitivity in this story is presented as a virtue to be cultivated and esteemed, not as a weakness.

Taking a spiritual perspective, the marriage of the princess and prince might represent the ultimate union of an individual with the Divine–enlightenment or salvation, if you will. The peace that prevails in the kingdom thereafter, together with happiness (we might assume), similarly alludes to the same concept.

That aside, Hans Christian Andersen chose to end his story with the words "this is a true story." The message of the importance of being authentic and finding our true selves is as true today as it's always been.

ACKNOWLEDGEMENTS

I would like to thank Heather McDonald for her kind assistance with proofreading and editing my original manuscript, Gucci and Goblin (two adorable cats) for serving as my muses and writing companions, and Graeme and Susan for allowing me to stay in their beautiful countryside retreat, where I was able to find the inspiration and peace to write. I'm grateful to Jacqueline Abromeit for help with cover formatting. Eternal thanks are due to The Great Creator, who inspires all ideas, and bestows the precious gifts of writing and storytelling.

The classical tales that are included in this book typically draw on more than one telling of each story. For the tales most associated with the Grimm brothers–*Little Red Riding Hood* and *The Sleeping Beauty*–I have generally followed their versions, rather than referring to earlier writings. The story of *Goldilocks and the three bears* is inspired by Robert Southey's original prose. Charles Perrault's version of *Jack and the beanstalk* provided the main source for my retelling of this colourful tale. *The princess and the pea* follows Hans Christian Andersen's masterwork. *Sinbad the porter and the second voyage of Sinbad the sailor* draws on the story as it was told in later compilations of *The thousand and one Arabian nights* canon. *The three little pigs* pays deference to the telling by James Halliwell-Phillipps.

The English words for *Stille Nacht* used in *Sleep in heavenly peace* are a translation from the original German lyrics of Joseph Mohr.

In the same series:

Arabian Nights & Arabian Nights–
Traditional tales from a thousand and one nights,
Contemporary tales for adults

ABOUT THE AUTHOR

Clive Johnson is a student and follower of the perennial tradition, the belief that many myths, fairy stories and faith traditions point to common truths at their heart. Clive is an interfaith minister ordained by the One Spirit Interfaith Foundation, as well as a teacher, storyteller and retreat host. He has had a lifelong interest in the power of myth and the oral tradition of story telling. Being autistic, a would-be mystic and not approaching his reflections from an academic standpoint, he approaches his writing with an open heart and a keen curiosity. He has no fixed home, pursuing a nomadic lifestyle that allows him to follow his heart. This is his sixth book.

Clive may be reached via his website, www.interfaithministry.co.uk.